THE BEAST C̶ ̶ ̶ ̶ ̶ ...

For several minutes, there was nothing but the hiss of the tape coursing past the recording head, and that damned dog. But then I heard a whispering sound, as if someone were talking *to himself* under his breath. It was close, and yet it seemed *far away* at the same time. *It was coming from the tank turret.*

Shaking and sweating, I knelt down beside the turret and tapped on it, twice. I sounded as choked up as a grade school kid after his first dry martini. I said: 'Who's there? Is there anybody inside there?'

There was a pause and then I heard a whispery voice say: '*You can help me, you know.*'

It was a strange voice, which seemed to come from everywhere at once. It seemed to have a smile in it as well; the kind of voice that someone has when they're secretly grinning. It could have been a man or a woman or a child, but I wasn't sure.

I said: 'Are you in there? Are you inside the tank?'

The voice whispered: '*You sound like a good man. A good man and true .* '

The Devils of D-Day

GRAHAM MASTERTON

Sphere Books Ltd

SPHERE BOOKS LIMITED

A Sphere Book

First published in Great Britain by Sphere Books Ltd 1979
Reprinted 1981 (twice), 1984, 1985, 1987, 1988, 1990

Printed and bound in Great Britain by
BPCC Hazell Books
Aylesbury, Bucks, England
Member of BPCC Ltd.

ISBN 0 7221 5993 5

Sphere Books Ltd
A Division of
Macdonald & Co (Publishers) Ltd
Orbit House,
1 New Fetter Lane,
London EC4A 1AR
A member of Maxwell Macmillan Pergamon Publishing Corporation

'The worst sort of devils are those who rejoice in wars and effusion of blood, and afflict men with most cruel stripes.'
— Francis Barrett

AUTHOR'S NOTE

All of the devils and demons that appear in this book are legendary creatures of hell, and there is substantial recorded evidence of their existence. For that reason, it is probably inadvisable to attempt to conjure up any of them by repeating out loud the incantations used in the text, which are also genuine.

I would like to point out that the Pentagon and the British Ministry of Defence strenuously deny the events described here, but I leave you to draw your own conclusions.

– Graham Masterton,
London, 1979

AUTHOR'S NOTE

All of the people and events that appear in this book are imaginary creations of full imagination, and any similar resemblance of their existence. The that reason it is probably unlikely for anyone to compute in any fashion by reporting or the plaintiffs used to the real whom me. So

Graham Masterton
London 1978

CHAPTER ONE

I could see them coming from almost a mile away: two small muffled figures on bicycles, their scarves wound tightly around their faces, pedalling between the white winter trees. As they came nearer, I could hear them talking, too, and make out the clouds of chilly vapour that clung around their mouths. It was Normandy in December – misty and grey as a photograph – and a sullen red sun was already sinking behind the forested hills. Apart from the two French labourers cycling slowly towards me, I was alone on the road, standing with my surveyor's tripod in the crisp frosted grass, my rented yellow Citroën 2CV parked at an ungainly angle on the nearby verge. It was so damned cold that I could hardly feel my hands or my nose, and I was almost afraid to stamp my feet in case my toes broke off.

The men came nearer. They were old, with donkey-jackets and berets, and one of them was carrying a battered army rucksack on his back with a long French loaf sticking out of it. Their bicycle tyres left white furry tracks on the hoar frost that covered the road. There wasn't much traffic along here, in the rural depths of the Suisse Normande, except for occasional tractors and even more occasional Citroën-Maseratis zipping past at ninety miles an hour in blizzards of ice.

I called, '*Bonjour, messieurs*,' and one of the old men slowed his bicycle and dismounted. He wheeled his machine right up to my tripod and said, '*Bonjour, monsieur, Qu'est-ce que vous faîtes?*'

I said, 'My French isn't too good. You speak English?'

The man nodded.

'Well,' I said, pointing across the valley towards the cold silvery hills, 'I'm making a map. *Une carte.*'

'*Ah, oui,*' said the old man. '*Une carte.*'

The other old man, who was still sitting astride his bicycle, pulled down his scarf from his face to blow his nose.

'It's for the new route?' he asked me. 'The new highway?'

'No, no. This is for someone's history book. It's a map of the whole of this area for a book about World War II.'

'*Ah, la guerre,*' nodded the first old man. '*Une carte de la guerre, hunh?*'

One of the men took out a blue packet of Gitanes, and offered me one. I didn't usually smoke French cigarettes, partly because of their high tar content and partly because they smelled like burning horsehair, but I didn't want to appear discourteous – not after only two days in northern France. In any case, I was glad of the spot of warmth that a glowing cigarette tip gave out.

We smoked for a while, and smiled at each other dumbly, the way people do when they can't speak each other's language too well. Then the old man with the loaf said, 'They fought all across this valley; and down by the river, too. The Orne. I remember it very clear.'

The other old man said: 'Tanks, you know? Here, and here. The Americans coming across the road from Clècy, and the Germans retreating back up the Orne valley. A very hard battle just there, you see, by the Pont D'Ouilly. But that day the Germans stood no chance. Those American tanks came across the bridge at Le Vey and cut them off. At night, from just here, you could see German tanks burning all the way up to the turn in the river.'

I blew out smoke and vapour. It was so gloomy now that I could hardly make out the heavy granite shoulders of the rocks at Ouilly, where the Orne river widened and turned before sliding over the dam at Le Vey and foaming northwards in the spectral December evening. The only sound was the faint rush of water, and the doleful tolling

2

of the church bell from the distant village, and out here in the frost and the cold we might just as well have been alone in the whole continent of Europe.

The old man with the loaf said, 'It was fierce, that fighting. I never saw it so fierce. We caught three Germans but it was no difficulty. They were happy to surrender. I remember one of them said: "Today, I fought the devil." '

The other old man nodded. '*Der Teufel*. That's what he said. I was there. This one and me, we're cousins.'

I smiled at them both. I didn't really know what to say.

'Well,' said the one with the loaf, 'we must get back for nourishment.'

'Thanks for stopping,' I told him. 'It gets pretty lonely standing out here on your own.'

'You're interested in the war?' asked the other old man.

I shrugged. 'Not specifically. I'm a cartographer. A map-maker.'

'There are many stories about the war. Some of them are just pipe-dreams. But round here there are many stories. Just down there, about a kilometre from the Pont D'Ouilly, there's an old American tank in the hedge. People don't go near it at night. They say you can hear the dead crew talking to each other inside it, on dark nights.'

'That's pretty spooky.'

The old man pulled up his scarf so that only his old wrinkled eyes peered out. He looked like a strange Arab soothsayer, or a man with terrible wounds. He tugged on his knitted gloves, and said, in a muffled voice, 'These are only stories. All battlefields have ghosts, I suppose. Anyway, *le potage s'attend*.'

The two old cousins waved once, and then pedalled slowly away down the road. It wasn't long before they turned a corner and disappeared behind the misty trees, and I was left on my own again, numb with cold and just about ready to pack everything away and grab some dinner. The sun was mouldering away behind a white wedge of descending fog now, anyway, and I could hardly see my hands in front of my face, let alone the peaks of distant rocks.

I stowed my equipment in the back of the 2CV, climbed into the driver's seat, and spent five minutes trying to get the car started. The damned thing whinnied like a horse, and I was just about to get out and kick it like a horse deserved, when it coughed and burst into life. I switched on the headlights, U-turned in the middle of the road, and drove back towards Falaise and my dingy hotel.

I was only about a half mile down the road, though, when I saw the sign that said *Pont D'Ouilly, 4 km.* I looked at my watch. It was only half past four, and I wondered if a quick detour to look at the old cousins' haunted tank might be worth while. If it was any good, I could take a photograph of it tomorrow, in daylight, and Roger might like it for his book. Roger Kellman was the guy who had written the history for which I was drawing all these maps, *The Days After D-Day*, and anything to do with military memorabilia would have him licking his lips like Sylvester the cat.

I turned off left, and almost immediately wished I hadn't. The road went sharply downhill, twisting and turning between trees and rocks, and it was slithery with ice, mud and half-frozen cowshit. The little Citroën bucked and swayed from side to side, and the windshield steamed up so much from my panicky breathing that I had to slide open the side window and lean out; and that wasn't much fun, with the outside temperature well down below freezing.

I passed silent, dilapidated farms, with sagging barns and closed windows. I passed grey fields in which cows stood like grubby brown-and-white jigsaws, frozen saliva

4

hanging from their hairy lips. I passed shuttered houses, and slanting fields that went down to the dark winter river. The only sign of life that I saw was a tractor, its wheels so caked with ochre clay that they were twice their normal size, standing by the side of the road with its motor running. There was nobody in it.

Eventually, the winding road took me down between rough stone walls, under a tangled arcade of leafless trees, and over the bridge at Ouilly. I kept a lookout for the tank the old cousins had talked about, but the first time I missed it altogether; and I spent five minutes wrestling the stupid car back around the way it had come, stalling twice and almost getting jammed in a farm gateway. In the greasy farmyard, I saw a stable door open, and an old woman with a grey face and a white lace cap stare out at me with suspicion, but then the door closed again, and I banged the 2CV into something resembling second gear and roared back down the road.

You could have missed the tank in broad daylight, let alone at dusk in the middle of a freezing Norman winter. Just as I came around the curve of the road, I saw it, and I managed to pull up a few yards away, with the Citroën's suspension complaining and groaning. I stepped out of the car into a cold pile of cow dung, but at least when it's chilled like that it doesn't smell. I scraped my shoe on a rock by the side of the road and then walked back to look at the tank.

It was dark and bulky, but surprisingly small. I guess we're so used to enormous Army tanks these days that we forget how tiny the tanks of World War II actually were. Its surface was black and scaly with rust, and it was so interwoven with the hedge that it looked like something out of Sleeping Beauty, with thorns and brambles twisted around its turret, laced in and out of its tracks, and wound around its stumpy cannon. I didn't know what kind of a tank it was, but I guessed it was maybe a Sherman or something like that. It was obviously Ameri-

5

can: there was a faded and rusted white star on its side, and a painting of some kind that time and the weather had just about obliterated. I kicked the tank, and it responded with a dull, empty booming sound.

A woman came walking slowly along the road with an aluminium milk pail. She eyed me cautiously as she approached, but as she drew near she stopped and laid down her pail. She was quite young, maybe twenty-three or twenty-four, and she wore a red spotted headscarf. She was obviously the farmer's daughter. Her hands were rough from pulling cows' udders in cold dawn barns, and her cheeks were bright crimson, like a painted peasant doll's. I said: '*Bonjour, mademoiselle*,' and she nodded in careful reply.

She said, 'You are American?'

'That's right.'

'I thought so. Only Americans stop and look.'

'You speak good English.'

She didn't smile. 'I was au-pair in England, in Pinner, for three years.'

'But then you came back to the farm?'

'My mother died. My father was all alone.'

I said, 'He has a loyal daughter.'

'Yes,' she said, lowering her eyes. 'But I expect I will go away again one day. It's very *solitaire* out here. Very lonesome.'

I turned back to the grim brooding bulk of the abandoned tank. 'I was told this was haunted,' I said. 'At night, you can hear the crew talking.'

The girl said nothing.

I waited for a while, and then turned again and looked across the road at her. 'Is that true, do you think?' I asked her. 'That it's haunted?'

'You mustn't speak about it,' she said. 'If you speak about it, it turns the milk.'

I glanced down at her aluminium pail. 'You're serious?

6

If you speak about the ghosts in the tank, the milk goes off?'

She whispered, 'Yes.'

I thought I'd heard everything, but this was amazing. Here, in modern France, an intelligent young lady was whispering in the presence of a beaten-up old Sherman tank, in case her fresh milk curdled. I rested my hand on the tank's cold rusted mudguard, and I felt as though I'd found something quite special. Roger would have adored it.

'Have you heard the ghosts yourself?' I asked her.

She quickly shook her head.

'Do you know anybody who has? Anybody I could speak to?'

She picked up her pail, and started to walk off down the road. But I crossed over and kept pace with her, even though she wouldn't look at me, and wouldn't answer.

'I don't want to be nosey, mam'selle. But we're getting a book together, all about D-Day and what happened afterwards. And this seems like the kind of story I could really use. I mean it. Surely someone's heard the voices, if they're real?'

She stopped walking, and stared at me hard. She was quite pretty for a Norman peasant. She had that straight nose you see on 11th-century women in the Bayeux tapestry, and opalescent green eyes. Underneath her mud-spattered jerkin and her sensible skirt and her rubber boots, she had quite a noticeable figure, too.

I said, 'I don't know what you've got to be so sensitive about. It's only a story, right? I mean, ghosts don't exist, right?'

She kept staring. Then she said, 'It's not a ghost, it's different from that.'

'What do you mean, different?'

'I can't tell you.'

She started walking again, and this time she walked so quickly I had difficulty keeping up. I guess if you walk

7

three miles to the cowsheds and back twice a day, your leg muscles get themselves built up pretty tough. By the time we'd reached the mossy stone gate where I'd turned my car round, I was wheezing for breath, and my throat was sore from the chill foggy air.

'This is my farm,' she said. 'I have to go in now.'

'You won't tell me any more?'

'There's nothing to tell. The tank has been there since the war. That's more than thirty years, isn't it? How could you hear voices in a tank after thirty years?'

'That's what I'm asking you,' I told her.

She turned her face away in profile. She had sad, curved lips; and with that straight aristocratic nose, she was almost beautiful. I said, 'Will you tell me your name?'

She gave a small, fleeting smile. 'Madeleine Passerelle. *Et vous?*'

'Dan, short for Daniel, McCook.'

The girl extended her hand, and we shook. 'I am pleased to have made your acquaintance,' she said. 'Now I must go.'

'Can I see you again? I'm up here again tomorrow. I have a map to finish.'

She shook her head.

'I'm not trying to pick you up,' I assured her. 'Maybe we could just go for a drink. Do you have a bar around here?'

I looked around at the cold soggy countryside, and the mournful cows gathering at the fence across the road.

'Well, maybe a small hotel?' I corrected myself.

Madeleine swung her pail of milk. 'I think I am too busy,' she said. 'And besides, my father needs a lot of care.'

'Who's the old woman?'

'Which old woman?'

'The old woman I saw at the stable door when I turned my car round. She had a white lace cap.'

8

'Oh . . . that's Eloise. She's lived at the farm all her life. She nursed my mother when she was sick. Now, *there's* someone to speak to if you're interested in stories about the tank. She believes in every superstition.'

I coughed in the cold twilight. 'Could I speak to her now?'

Madeleine said, 'Not tonight. Perhaps another day.'

She turned, and started to walk across the farmyard, but I caught up with her and grabbed the handle of her milking pail. 'Listen, how about tomorrow?' I asked her. 'I could come around noon. Could you spare a few minutes then?'

I was determined not to let her get away without making some kind of firm commitment. The tank and its ghosts were pretty interesting, but Madeleine Passerelle herself was even more so. You don't usually get much action when you're drawing up a military map of northern France, and a few glasses of wine and a tumble in the cowshed with the farmer's daughter, even in the deep midwinter, was a lot more appealing than silent and solitary meals in the brown garlic-smelling mausoleum that my hotel jocularly called its dining room.

Madeleine smiled. 'Very well. Come and eat with us. But make it at eleven-thirty. We lunch early in France.'

'You've made my week. Thanks a lot.'

I reached forward to kiss her, but my foot slid on the churned-up mud of the farmyard, and I almost lost my balance. I saved most of my dignity by turning my slide into three rapid steps, but the kiss was lost to the freezing air, a puff of vapour that vanished in the dusk. Amused, Madeleine said, '*Au revoir*, M. McCook. Until tomorrow.'

I watched her walk across the yard and disappear through the stable door. A cold wet drizzle was beginning to sift down from the evening sky, and it would probably turn into snow in an hour or two. I left the farm and began to trudge back down the road towards the Pont D'Ouilly, where I'd left my car.

9

Along the road, it was silent and soaking and dark. I kept my hands shoved deep in my overcoat pockets and my scarf pulled up over my mouth. Way over to my right, I could hear the Orne rushing over the brownish granite rocks of its shallow bed, and on my left, just beyond the hedge, reared the slabby blocks of the cliffs that gave this part of Normandy its name – Swiss Normandy. The rocks were jacketed in slime and moss, and laced up with hanging tree-roots, and you could just imagine strange and malignant creatures lurking in their crevices and cracks.

I hadn't realised how far I'd walked along the road with Madeleine. It took me almost five minutes before I saw my yellow car by the verge, and the huddled black bulk of the abandoned tank. The drizzle was turning into large wet flakes of half-melted snow now, and I pulled my coat collar up and walked more quickly.

Who knows what odd tricks your eyes can play in the snow and the dark? When your eyes are tired, you can see dark shadows like cats slipping away at the corner of your field of vision. Shadows can seem to stand on their own, and trees can seem to move. But that evening, on the road to Pont D'Ouilly, I was sure that my eyes weren't playing up, and that I did see something. There's a French road sign which warns that the night can deceive you, and possibly it did, but I still think that what I glimpsed wasn't an optical illusion. It was enough to make me stop in the road, and feel a tight chill that was even colder than the evening air.

Through the tumbling snow, a few yards away from the derelict tank, I saw a small bony figure, white in the darkness, not much taller than a child of five, and it seemed to be hopping or running. The sight of it was so sudden and strange that I was momentarily terrified; but then I ran forward through the snow and shouted, 'Hey! You!'

My shout echoed flatly back from the nearby rocks. I

peered into the dark but there was nobody there. Only the rusting bulk of the Sherman tank, woven into the brambles of the hedge. Only the wet road, and the noise of the river. There was no sign of any figure; no sign of any child. I walked back across to my car and checked it for damage, in case the figure had been a vandal or a thief, but the Citroën was unmarked. I climbed thoughtfully inside and sat there for a minute or two drying my face and hair with my handkerchief, wondering what the hell was going on around here.

I started the Citroën's engine, but just before I drove off I took one last look at the tank. It gave me a really peculiar feeling, thinking that it had been decaying by this roadside since 1944, unmoved, and that here at this very place the American Army had fought to liberate Normandy. For the first time in my map-making career, I felt history was alive; I felt history move under my feet. I wondered if the skeletons of the crew were still inside the tank, but I decided that they'd probably been taken out years ago and given a decent burial. The French were beautifully and gravely respectful to the remains of the men who had died trying to liberate them.

I released the Citroën's brake and drove down the gloomy road, across the bridge, and back up the winding hill to the main highway. The snow was crowding my windshield, and the car's tacky little windshield wipers were having about as much success in clearing it away as two geriatrics sweeping up the ticker-tape after Lindy's parade through Wall Street. When I joined the main stream of traffic, I almost collided with a Renault which was bombing through the snow at eighty-five. *Vive la vélocité*, I thought to myself, as I crawled back towards Falaise at twenty.

Next day, in the high-ceilinged hotel dining room, I ate a solemn breakfast of croissants and coffee and confitures, watching myself in the mottled mirrors and trying to decipher what the hell was happening in the world today from a copy of *Le Figaro* on a long stick. Across the room, a rotund Frenchman with waxed whiskers and a huge white napkin tucked in his shirt collar was wolfing down breadrolls as though he was trying to put up the price of shares in the bakery industry. A waitress in black with a pinched face rapped around the black-and-white tiled floor in court shoes and made sure you felt you were lonely and unwanted, and that you only wanted breakfast because you were an unpardonable pest. I thought of changing hotels, but then I thought of Madeleine, and things didn't seem too bad.

I spent most of the morning on the new curve of road that comes into Clécy from the south-east. A dry wind had lifted away most of the snow during the night, but it was still intensely cold, and the village lay frosted in its valley, with the broad hump of the hills far behind it, and tiny villagers came and went from its doors, tending their gardens or their washing, or fetching in logs, and the hours rang from the tall church spire, and New York seemed a very long way away.

Maybe my mind was distracted, but I only managed to finish half the readings that I'd hoped to take, and by eleven o'clock, as the church tolled its hour, I was wrapped up and ready to drive across to Pont D'Ouilly I'd taken the trouble to stop at a store in the village and buy a very reasonable bottle of Bordeaux, just in case Madeleine's father needed a little appeasing. I also bought, for Madeleine herself, a box of crystallised fruit. They're very big on crystallised fruit in Normandy.

The rented Citroën coughed and choked, but finally found its way down the twisting road to the bridge. The countryside didn't look very much more hospitable by daylight than it had by night. There was a cold silvery haze over the fields, and mist was hanging under the elms like soiled net curtains. The cows were still there, standing patiently in the chill, chewing the colourless grass and breathing out so much steam they looked like roomfuls of heavy smokers. I drove over the stone bridge, with the Orne gargling beneath me, and then I slowed down so that I could take a look at the tank.

There it was – silent and broken – wound in brambles and leafless creeper. I stopped the car for a moment and slid open my window so that I could see the corroded wheels, the collapsed tracks, and the small dark turret with its scaly sides. There was something deeply sinister and sorrowful about it. It reminded me of the abandoned Mulberry harbour that still lies off the shore of Arromanches, on Normandy's channel coast, a grim memorial to June 6, 1944, that no stone monument or statue could ever adequately replace.

I looked around at the dank hedgerow for a while, and then I started the car up again and drove along to Madeleine's farm. I turned into the gate and splashed across the muddy yard, with chickens flapping and skittering all around me, and a flock of grubby geese rushing away like athletes on a cross-country run.

I stepped out of the car, being careful where I put my feet, and reached in for my presents. A door opened behind me, and I heard someone walking my way. A voice said, '*Bonjour, monsieur. Qu'est-ce que vous voulez?*'

A short Frenchman in muddy pants, muddy boots and a muddy brown jacket was standing in the yard with his hands in his pockets. He had a long Norman face, and he was smoking a Gauloise that appeared to be permanently stuck to his lip. His beret was pulled well down to his ears, which made him look pretty rural, but his eyes were bright and he looked like the kind of farmer who didn't miss a trick.

'My name's Dan McCook,' I told him. 'Your daughter Madeleine invited me for lunch. Er – *pour déjeuner?*'

The farmer nodded. 'Yes, monsieur. She tells me this. I am Jacques Passerelle.'

We shook hands. I offered him the bottle of wine, and

13

said, 'I brought you this. I hope you like it. It's a bordeaux.'

Jacques Passerelle paused for a moment, and reached in his breast pocket for a pair of wire-rimmed spectacles. He hooked them around his ears, and scrutinised the bottle closely. I felt as if I'd had the down-right effrontery to give a vacuum pack of A&P bacon to a Kentucky hog farmer. But the Frenchman nodded again, put away his spectacles, and said, '*Merci bien, monsieur*. I save this for *dimanche*.'

He ushered me through the stable door into the kitchen. The old woman Eloise was there, in her dark grey dress and her white lace cap, boiling a huge copper pan full of apples. Jacques introduced me, and we shook hands. Her fingers were soft and dry, and she was wearing a silver ring with a miniature Bible on it. She had one of those flat, pale, wrinkled faces that you sometimes see staring out of the windows of old people's homes, or from the windows of buses on old people's outings. But she seemed to be independent and strong around the Passerelle home, and she walked with a stright back.

She said, 'Madeleine told me you were interested in the tank.'

I glanced at Jacques, but he didn't seem to be listening. I coughed, and said, 'Sure. I'm making a map of these parts for a book about D-Day.'

'The tank has been here since July, 1944. Mid-July. It died on a very hot day.'

I looked at her. Her eyes were washed-out blue, like the sky after a spring shower, and you didn't quite know whether she was looking inwards or outwards. I said, 'Maybe we can talk after lunch.'

Out of the steamy, apple-aromatic kitchen, we walked along a narrow dark hallway with a bare boarded floor Jacques opened a door in the side of the hall, and said 'You would care for an aperitif?'

This was obviously his front parlour, the room he kept only for visitors. It was gloomy, heavily-curtained, and it smelled of dust and stale air and furniture polish. There were three chintz armchairs in the style you can see in any large French *meubles* store, a copper warming-pan hanging on the wall, a plastic madonna with a small container of holy water, and a dark-varnished sideboard with photographs of weddings and grandchildren, each on its own lace doily. A tall clock ticked away the winter morning, weary and slow.

'I'd like a calvados, please,' I told Jacques. 'I don't know anything better for warming yourself up on a cold day. Not even Jack Daniels.'

Jacques took two small glasses from the sideboard, uncorked the calvados, and poured it out. He handed one over, and lifted his own glass solemnly.

'*Santé*,' he said quietly, and downed his drink in one gulp.

I sipped mine more circumspectly. Calvados, the apple-brandy of Normany, is potent stuff, and I did want to do some sensible work this afternoon.

'You have been here in summer?' asked Jacques.

'No, never. This is only my third trip to Europe.'

'It's not so pleasant in winter. The mud, and the frost. But in summer, this is very beautiful. We have visitors from all over France, and Europe. You can hire boats and row along the river.'

'It sounds terrific. Do you have many Americans?'

Jacques shrugged. 'One or two. Some Germans sometimes, too. But not many come here. Pont D'Ouilly is still a painful memory. The Germans ran away from here as if the devil himself were after them.'

I swallowed some more calvados, and it glowed down my throat like a shovelful of hot coke. 'You're the second person who's said that,' I told him. '*Der Teufel*.'

Jacques gave a small smile, which reminded me of the way that Madeleine smiled.

15

'I must change my clothes,' he said. 'I don't like to sit down for lunch looking like a mud man.'

'Go ahead,' I told him. 'Will Madeleine be down?'

'In a moment. She wanted to put on cosmetics. Well . . . we don't have many visitors.'

Jacques went off to clean himself up, and I went over to the window and looked out across the orchard. The fruit trees were all bare now, and pruned, and the grass was white with cold. A bird perched for a moment on the rough fence of silver-birch at the far end of the garden, and then fluttered off. I turned back into the room.

On the sideboard, one of the photographs showed a young girl with a wavy 1940s hairstyle, and I guessed that must have been Madeleine's mother. There was a colour picture of Madeleine as a baby, with a smiling priest in the background, and a formal portrait of Jacques in a high white collar. Besides all these was a bronze model of a medieval cathedral, with a ring of twisted hair around its spire. I couldn't really work out what that was supposed to mean, but then I wasn't a Roman Catholic, and I wasn't really into religious relics.

I was just about to pick up the model to take a better look when the parlour door opened. It was Madeleine, in a pale cream cotton dress, her dark-blonde hair brushed back and held with tortoiseshell combs, her lips bright red with lipstick.

'Please—' she said. 'Don't touch that.'

I raised my hands away from the tiny cathedral. 'I'm sorry. I was only going to take a look.'

'It's something of my mother's.'

'I'm sorry.'

'That's all right. Don't think about it. Did father give you a drink?'

'Sure. A calvados. It's making my ears ring already. Are you going to join me?'

She shook her head. 'I can't drink it. They gave it to

16

me once when I was twelve and I was sick. Now, I only drink wine.'

She sat down, and I sat opposite. 'You shouldn't have dressed up specially for me,' I told her. 'But all the same, you look beautiful.'

She blushed. Not much, just a small tinge on the cheeks, but it was a blush all right. I hadn't come across that kind of modesty for years.

I said, 'I had a real weird experience last night. I was walking back to my car, and I could have sworn I saw something on the road.'

She looked up. 'What was it?'

'Well, I'm not too sure. It was like a small child, but it was too thin and bony for a small child.'

She looked at me for several silent seconds. Then she said, 'I don't know. It must have been the snow.'

'It scared the hell out of me, whatever it was.'

She picked absentmindedly at the braiding on the arm of her chair. 'It's the atmosphere, the *ambience*, around the tank. It makes people feel things, see things, that aren't there. Eloise will tell you some of the stories if you want.'

'You don't believe them yourself?'

She shrugged. 'What's the use? All you do is frighten yourself. I'd rather think of real things, not of ghosts and spirits.'

I put down my glass on the small side-table. 'I get the feeling you don't like it here.'

'Here, in my father's house?'

'No – in Pont D'Ouilly. It's not exactly the entertainment centre of northern France, is it?'

Madeleine stood up and walked across to the window. Against the grey winter light, she was a soft dark silhouette. She said, 'I don't think so much of entertainment. If you've lived here, in Pont D'Ouilly, then you know what sadness is, and anything at all is better than sadness.'

'Don't tell me you loved and lost.'

She smiled. 'I suppose you could say that. I loved life and I lost my love of life.'

I said, 'I'm not sure I understand.' But at that moment, a gong rang from across the hall, and Madeleine turned and said, 'Lunch is ready. We'd better go in.'

Today, we had lunch in the dining room, although I suspected that they usually ate in the kitchen, especially when they had three inches of mud on their boots and appetites like horses. Eloise had set out a huge tureen of hot brown onion soup on the oval table, with crisp garlic bread, and I suddenly realised that I was starved of home cooking. Jacques was already standing at the head of the table in a neatly-pressed brown suit, and when we had all taken our seats, he bowed his thinning scalp towards us, and said grace.

'Oh Lord, who provides all that we eat, thank you for this nourishment. And protect us from the conversations of evil, in the name of the Father, and of the Son, and of the Holy Spirit, amen.'

I looked across the table at Madeleine, and tried to put the question in my eyes. *The conversations of evil?* What was that all about? The voices in the tank? Or what? But Madeleine's attention was fastened on the large tureen, as Eloise dished up piping-hot platefuls of transparent brown soup, and whether she intended to avoid my gaze of not, she didn't look up again until her father had started to talk.

'The upper field is frozen,' he said, dabbing his lips with his napkin. 'I ploughed a hectare this morning, and there was ice coming up with the soil. It hasn't been so cold here for ten years.'

Eloise said, 'There are worse winters to come. The dogs know it.'

'The dogs?' I asked her.

'That's right, monsieur. When a dog stays close to

home, and when he calls in the night, that's when the nights will grow cold for three years, one after another.'

'You believe that? Or is that just a French country saying?'

Eloise frowned at me. 'It is nothing to do with belief. It is true. I have seen it happen for myself.'

Jacques put in: 'Eloise has a way with nature, Mr McCook. She can heal you with dandelion broth, or send you to sleep with burdock and thyme.'

'Can she exorcise ghosts?'

Madeleine breathed, 'Dan—' but Eloise was not put out. She examined me with those watery old eyes of hers, and almost smiled.

'I hope you don't think I'm impertinent,' I said. 'But it seems to me that everybody around here is kind of anxious about that tank, and if you could exorcise it . . .'

Eloise slowly shook her head. 'Only a priest can exorcise,' she said gently, 'and the only priest who will believe us is too old and too weak for such things.'

'You really believe it's haunted?'

'It depends on what you mean by "haunted", monsieur.'

'Well, as far as I can make out, the dead crew are supposed to be heard talking to each other at night. Is that it?'

'Some say that,' said Jacques.

I glanced at him. 'And what do others say?'

'Others will not talk about it at all.'

Eloise spooned up her soup carefully. 'Nobody knows much about the tanks. But they were not like the usual American tanks. They were different, very different, and Father Anton, our priest, said they were visitations from *l'enfer*, from hell itself.'

Madeleine said, 'Eloise – do we have to talk about it? We don't want to spoil the lunch.'

But Eloise raised her hand. 'It doesn't matter. This

young man wants to know about the tank, then why shouldn't he?'

I said: 'How were they different? It looks like a regular tank to me.'

'Well,' explained Eloise, 'they were painted black all over, although you cannot see that now, because the rust and the weather have taken away the paint. There were thirteen of them. I know, because I counted them as they came along the road from Le Vey. Thirteen, on the thirteenth day of July. But what was most strange, they never opened their turrets. Most American tanks came with their tops open, and the soldiers would throw us candy and cigarettes and nylon stockings. But these tanks came and we never saw who drove them. They were always closed.'

Madeleine had finished her soup and was sitting upright in her chair. She looked very pale, and it was clear that all this talk about the strange tanks disconcerted her. I said, 'Did you talk to any Americans about them? Did they ever tell you what they were?'

Jacques, with his mouth full of garlic bread, said, 'They didn't know, or they wouldn't speak. They just said "special division", and that was all.'

'Only one was left behind,' put in Eloise. 'That was the tank which is still there, down the road. It broke a track and stopped. But the Americans did nothing to take it away. Instead, they came along next day and welded down the turret. Yes, they welded it, and then an English priest came and said words over it, and it was left to rot.'

'You mean the crew was left inside?'

Jacques tore off some more bread. 'Who can say? They wouldn't let anyone near. I have talked many times to the police and to the mayor, and all they say is that the tank is not to be moved. And there it stays.'

Madeleine said, 'And ever since it's been there, the village has been dead and depressed.'

'Because of the voices?'

20

Madeleine shrugged. 'There have been voices. At least, that's what some people say. But more than anything else, it's the tank itself. It's a terrible reminder of something that most of us now would prefer to forget.'

Eloise said, 'Those tanks could not be stopped. They set fire to German tanks all along the river, and then they set fire to the Germans themselves who tried to escape from them. You could hear the screams all night of men burning. In the morning, the tanks were gone. Who knows where, or how? But they came through in one day and one night, and nothing on earth could have held them back. I know they saved us, *monsieur*, but I still shudder when I think of them.'

'Who's heard these voices? Do they know what they say?'

Eloise said, 'Not many people walk along that road at night any more. But Madame Verrier said she heard whispering and laughter, one night in February; and old Henriques told of voices that boomed and shouted. I myself have carried milk and eggs past that tank, and the milk has soured and the eggs have gone rotten. Gaston from the next farm had a terrier which sniffed around the tank, and the dog developed tremors and shakes. Its hair fell out, and after three days it died. Everybody has one story about the evil that befalls you if you go too near the tank; and so these days nobody does.'

I said, 'Isn't it just superstition? I mean, there's no real evidence.'

'You should ask Father Anton,' said Eloise. 'If you are really foolhardy enough to want to know more, Father Anton will probably tell you. The English priest who said words over the tank stayed at his house for a month, and I know they spoke of the tank often. Father Anton was never happy that it was left by the road, but there was nothing he could do, short of carrying it away on his own back.'

Madeleine said, 'Please let's talk about other things. The war is so depressing.'

'Okay,' I said, lifting my hands in mock surrender. 'But thank you for what you've told me. It's going to make a real good story. Now, I'd love some more of that onion soup.'

Eloise smiled. 'You have a big appetite, monsieur. I remember the American appetites.'

She ladled out more of that scalding brown soup, while Madeleine and her father watched me with friendly caution, and a little bit of suspicion, and maybe the hope that I wasn't really going to bother to do anything unsettling, like talk to Father Anton about what happened on July 13, 1944, on the road from Le Vey.

After lunch of hare casserole, with good red wine and fruit, we sat around the table and smoked Gauloises and Jacques told me stories of his boyhood at Pont D'Ouilly. Madeleine came and sat beside me, and it was plain that she was getting to like me. Eloise retreated to the kitchen, and clattered pans, but returned fifteen minutes later with tiny cups of the richest coffee I'd ever tasted.

At last, at well past three o'clock, I said: 'I've had a marvellous time, but I have to get back to work. I have a whole mess of readings to take before it gets dark.'

'It's been good to talk with you,' said Jacques, standing up and giving a small bow. 'It isn't often we have people to eat with us. I suppose we are too close to the tank, and people don't like to come this way.'

'It's that bad?'

'Well, it isn't comfortable.'

While Madeleine helped to take out the last dishes, and Jacques went to open the farm gate for me, I stood in the kitchen buttoning my coat and watching Eloise's bent back as she washed up over the steamy sink.

I said, '*Au revoir*, Eloise.'

She didn't turn round, but she said, '*Au revoir, monsieur.*'

I took a step towards the back door, but then I paused, and looked at her again. 'Eloise?' I asked.

'*Oui, monsieur?*'

'What is it really, inside that tank?'

I saw the almost imperceptible stiffening of her back. The mop stopped slapping against the plates, and the knives and forks stopped clattering.

She said, 'I do not know, *monsieur*. Truly.'

'Have a guess.'

She was silent for a moment. Then she said, 'Perhaps it is nothing at all. But perhaps it is something that neither heaven nor earth knows anything about.'

'That only leaves hell.'

Again, she was silent. Then she turned from the sink and looked at me with those pale, wise eyes.

'*Oui, monsieur. Et le roi de l'enfer, c'est le diable.*'

The priest was very old. He must have been almost ninety, and he sat at his dusty leather-topped desk like a sagging sack of soft potatoes. But he had an intelligent, kindly face; and even though he spoke slowly and softly, as his lungs filled and emptied with the laboured aspiration of ancient bellows, he was lucid in his words, and precise. He had fraying white hair and a bony nose you could have hung your hat on, and as he talked he had a habit of steepling his long fingers and lifting his neck so that he could see down into the grey cobbled courtyard that fronted his house.

He said, 'The English cleric's name was the Reverend Taylor,' and he peered out of the window as if expecting the Reverend Taylor to appear around the corner at any moment.

'The Reverend Taylor? There must be five thousand Reverend Taylors in England.'

Father Anton smiled, and did something complicated inside his mouth with his dentures. 'That is probably so.

23

But I am quite certain that there is only one Reverend Woodfall Taylor.'

It was four-thirty now, almost dark, but I had got so caught up in the mystery of this decaying Sherman that I had skipped my cartographic readings for the day, and taken a trip up to the opposite end of the village to talk to Father Anton. He lived in a huge, sombre, forbidding French house in the severest style, with a hall of dark polished wood that you could have landed a 747 on, and staircase after staircase of chilled marble, flanked by gloomy oil paintings of cardinals and Popes and other miserable doyens of the church. Everywhere you looked, there was a mournful face. It was as bad as spending the evening at a Paul Robeson record night in Peoria, Illinois.

Father Anton said, 'When he came here, Mr Taylor was a very enthusiastic young vicar. He was full of the energy of religion. But I don't think he truly understood the importance of what he had to do. I don't think he understood how terrible it was, either. Without being unkind, I think he was the kind of young cleric who is easily seduced into thinking that mysticism is the firework display that celebrates true faith. Mind you, the Americans paid him a great deal of money. It was enough to build himself a new steeple, and a church hall. You can't blame him.'

I coughed. It was wickedly cold in Father Anton's house, and apart from saving on heating he also seemed to have a penchant for penny-pinching on electricity. The room was so shadowy and dark that I could barely make him out, and all I could see distinctly was the shine of the silver crucifix around his neck.

I said, 'What I don't understand is why we needed him. What was he doing for us, anyway?'

'He never clearly explained, monsieur. He was gagged by your oaths of secrecy. Apart from that, I don't think he truly understood himself what it was he was required to do.'

'But the tanks – the black tanks—'

The old priest turned towards me, and I could just make out the rheumy gleam of his eye.

'The black tanks were something about which I cannot speak, *monsieur*. I have done all that I can for thirty long years, to have the tank taken away from Pont D'Ouilly but each time I have been told that it is too heavy, and that it is not economical to tow it away. But I think the truth is that they are too frightened to disturb it.'

'Why should they be frightened?'

Father Anton opened his desk drawer and took out a small rosewood and silver snuffbox. He asked, 'You take snuff?'

'No, thanks. But I wouldn't mind a cigarette.'

He passed me the cigarette box, and then snorted two generous pinches of snuff up his cavernous nostrils. I always thought people sneezed after they took snuff, but all Father Anton did was snort like a mule, and relax further into his creaky revolving chair.

I lit my cigarette and said, 'Is there something still *inside* that tank?'

Father Anton thought about this, and then answered. 'Perhaps. I don't know what. The Reverend Taylor would never speak about it, and when they sealed down the turret, nobody from the whole village was allowed within half a kilometre.'

'Did they give any kind of explanation?'

'Yes,' said Father Anton. 'They said there was high explosive inside it, and that there was some danger of a blast. But of course none of us believed it. Why should they need a vicar to sanctify the sealing of a few pounds of TNT?'

'So you believe that tank has something unholy about it?'

'It's not what *I* believe, *monsieur*. It's what your Army obviously believed, and I have yet to meet anyone more sceptical than a soldier. Why should an Army call in a

25

cleric to deal with its weapons? I can only assume that there was something about the tank that was not in accordance with the laws of God.'

I wasn't entirely sure what he meant by that, but the slow and lisping way in which he said it, the way the words came out in that freezing and sepulchral room like dead flowers, that was enough to make me feel chilled and strangely frightened.

I said, 'Do you believe in the voices?'

Father Anton nodded. 'I have heard them myself. Anyone brave enough to go near the tank after dark can hear them.'

'You heard them yourself?'

'Not officially.'

'How about unofficially?'

The old priest wiped at his nose with his handkerchief. 'Unofficially, of course, I *made* it my business. I last visited the tank three or four years ago, and spent several hours there in prayer. It didn't do my rheumatism a great deal of good, but I am sure now that the tank is an instrument of evil works.'

'Did you hear anything distinct? I mean, what kind of voices were they?'

Father Anton chose his next sentence with care. 'They were not, in my opinion, the voices of men.'

I frowned at him. 'I don't understand.'

'*Monsieur*, what can I tell you? They were not the voices of human spirits or of human ghosts.'

I didn't know what to say after that. We sat in silence for a few minutes, and outside the day grew grainier and darker, tinged with that corroded green that always threatened snow. Father Anton seemed to be deeply buried in thought, but after a time he raised his head and said, 'Is that all, *monsieur*? I have studies to continue.'

'Well, I guess so. The whole thing seems like a real mystery.'

'The ways of war are always a mystery, *monsieur*. I

have heard many stories of strange and inexplicable events on battlefields, or in the concentration camps. Sometimes, holy miracles occur, visitations by saints. I have a parishioner who fought at the Somme, and he swears he was visited every night by Saint Thérèse. Then again, monsters and agents of hell have been seen, seeking out the cowardly and the vicious. It was said that Heinrich Reutemann, the SS commandant, kept at Dachau a dog that was possessed by the devil.'

'And this tank?'

The pale withered hands formed their reverent steeple. 'Who knows, *monsieur*? It is beyond my comprehension.'

I thanked him, and got up to leave. His room was like a dark musty cave. I said, 'Do you think it's dangerous?'

He didn't turn his head. 'The manifestations of evil are always dangerous, my friend. But the greatest protection from evil is a steadfast belief in Our Lord.'

I stood by the door for a moment, straining my eyes to see him through the gloom. 'Yes,' I said and then went down the cold and silent marble staircases to the front door, and out into the wintry street.

I didn't drive straight there, partly because I was waiting for the late afternoon to grow darker, and partly because the whole thing made me unusually nervous. By seven o'clock, though, after a roundabout tour through the muddy shuttered villages of the *Route Scenique* of the Orne Valley; past farmyards and peeling houses and roadside shrines where pale effigies of Christ crucified leaned mournfully into the evening frost; past inkblot trees and cold whispering fields; I arrived at the Passerelle's farm, and drove into the yard.

The evening was bitter and still when I climbed out of the Citroën and walked across to the farmhouse door. A dog was yapping at some other farm, way across the valley; but here everything was quiet. I knocked on the door and waited.

27

Madeleine came to the door. She was wearing a blue check cowboy shirt and jeans, and she looked as if she'd just finished changing a wheel on a tractor.

'Dan,' she said, but she didn't sound surprised. 'You left something here?'

'No, no. I came back for you.'

'For me? *Je ne comprends pas.*'

I said, 'Can I come in? It's like the North Pole out here. I only wanted to ask you something.'

'Of course,' she told me, and opened the door wider.

The kitchen was warm and empty. I sat down at the broad pine table, scarred from a hundred years of knives and hot saucepans, and she went across to the corner cupboard and poured me a small glass of brandy. Then she sat down opposite, and said, 'Are you still thinking about the tank?'

'I went to see Father Anton.'

She smiled faintly. 'I thought you would.'

'Am I that easy to read?'

'I don't think so,' she smiled. 'But you seem like the kind of man who doesn't like to leave puzzles unsolved. You make maps, so your whole life is spent unravelling mysteries. And this one, of course, is a very special enigma indeed.'

I sipped my brandy. 'Father Anton says he's heard the voices himself.'

She stared down at the table. Her finger traced the pattern of a flower that had been scorched into the wood by a hot fish-kettle. She commented, 'Father Anton is very old.'

'You mean he's senile?'

'I don't know. But his sermons ramble these days. Perhaps he could have imagined these things.'

'Maybe he could. But I'd still like to find out for myself.'

She glanced up. 'You want to hear them for yourself?'

'Certainly. I'd like to make a tape-recording, too. Has anyone ever thought of doing that?'

'Dan – not many people have ever gone to listen to the voices on purpose.'

'No, I know that. But that's what I want to do tonight. And I was hoping you'd come along with me.'

She didn't answer straight away, but stared across the kitchen as if she was thinking of something quite different. Her hair was tied back in a knot, which didn't suit her too much, but then I guess a girl doesn't worry too much about the charisma of her coiffure when she's mucking out cows. Almost unconsciously, she crossed herself, and then she looked back at me. 'You really want to go?'

'Well, sure. There has to be some kind of explanation.'

'Americans always need explanations?'

I finished my brandy, and shrugged. 'I guess it's a national characteristic. In any case, I was born and bred in Mississippi.'

Madeleine bit her lip. She said, 'Supposing I asked you not to go?'

'Well, you can ask me. But I'd have to say that I'm going anyway. Listen, Madeleine, there's a fascinating story in this. There's some kind of weird thing going on in that old tank and I want to know what it is.'

'*C'est malin*,' she said. 'It is wicked.'

I reached across the old table and laid my hand over hers. 'That's what everybody says, but so far I haven't seen anything that proves it. All I want to do is find out what the voices are saying, if there are any voices, and then we can go from there. I mean, I can't say that I'm not scared. I think it's very scary. But a whole lot of scarey things turn out to be real interesting once you take the trouble to check them out.'

'Dan, please. It's more than simply scarey.'

'How can you say that unless you investigate it?' I asked her. 'I don't knock superstition, but here's a superstition we can actually test for ourselves.'

She took back her hand, and crossed her arms across her breasts as if to protect herself from the consequences of what she was about to say. 'Dan,' she whispered. 'The tank killed my mother.'

I raised an eyebrow. 'The tank did *what*?'

'It killed my mother. Well, it was responsible. Father isn't sure, but Eloise knows it, and I know it. I have never told anyone else, but then nobody else has shown such interest in the tank as you. I have to warn you, Dan. Please.'

'How could the tank have killed your mother? It doesn't move, does it? The guns don't fire?'

She turned her elegant Norman profile away from me, and spoke in a steady, modulated whisper. 'It was last year, late in summer. Five of our herd died from disease. Mother said it was the tank that had done it. She always blamed the tank for everything that went wrong. If it rained and our hay rotted she would blame the tank. Even if one of her cakes wouldn't rise. But last year she said she was going to fix the tank for ever. Eloise tried to persuade her to leave it alone, but she wouldn't listen. She went down the road with holy water, sprinkled it across the tank, and spoke the dismissal of demons.'

'The dismissal of demons? What the hell's that?'

Madeleine touched her forehead. 'The words of exorcism. Mother always believed in devils and demons, and she has the words in one of her holy books.'

'Well, what happened?'

Madeleine slowly shook her head. 'She was only a simple woman. She was kind and she was loving and she believed deeply in God and the Virgin Mary. Yet her religion couldn't save her. Thirteen days after she sprinkled the holy water on the tank, she started to cough blood, and she died in hospital in Caen after a week. The doctors said she had some form of tuberculosis, but they could never say precisely what form it was, or why she had died so quickly.'

30

I felt embarrassed now, as well as afraid. 'I'm sorry.' Madeleine looked up, and there was that wry smile again. 'You have no need to be. But you can see why I'd rather you didn't go near the tank.'

I thought for a while. It would be easy enough to forget the tank altogether, or simply add a footnote to Roger's book that the last remaining Sherman tank of a secret special division was still decaying in the Norman countryside, and that local yokels believed it was possessed by evil. But how can you dismiss something like that as a footnote? I didn't particularly believe in demons and devils, but here was a whole French village that was scared half to death, and a girl seriously claiming that malevolent spirits had deliberately killed her mother.

I pushed back my chair and stood up. 'I'm sorry,' I said, 'but I'm still going to take a look. If it's true, what you said about your mother, then we've got the biggest supernatural story here since Uri Geller.'

'Uri Geller?' she frowned.

I coughed. 'He, er, bends spoons.'

She sat at the table looking a little sad. Then she said: 'Well, if you *insist* on going, I'll have to come with you. I don't want you to go on your own.'

'Madeleine, if it's really that dangerous—'

'I'll come with you, Dan,' she repeated firmly, and all I could do was lift my hands in acceptance. I was glad of the company anyway.

While I turned the 2CV around in the yard, Madeleine went to get her overcoat. The clouds were beginning to clear a little, and there was a washed-out moon up above us like a white-faced boy peering through a dirty window. Madeleine crossed the yard, climbed into the car, and we bounced off across the ruts and the puddles until we reached the road. Just before we turned, Madeleine reached over and squeezed my hand. 'I would like to say, "good luck," ' she whispered.

'Thanks,' I told her. 'And the same to you.'

31

It took us two or three minutes to reach the hedge where the tank lay entangled. As soon as I saw the shape of it, I pulled the Citroën over on to the opposite verge, and killed the motor. I lifted my battery-operated tape recorder out of the back seat, and opened the car door.

Madeleine said: 'I'll wait here. Just for the moment, anyway. Call me if you need me.'

'Okay.'

Down here by the river, under the brow of the cliffs, the pallid moonlight barely reached. I crossed the road and stepped right up to the tank, touching its cold corroded mudguard. It seemed so dead and desolate and rusted that, now I saw it again for real, it was hard to believe that there was anything supernatural about it. It was nothing more than the abandoned junk of war.

There was a rustling sound in the grass around the tracks, and I froze. But then a rabbit jumped out from underneath the tank, and scampered off into the hedge. It was kind of late in the year for rabbits, but I guess they could have made their nest inside the tank itself, or underneath it somewhere. Maybe that was the real answer to Pont D'Ouilly's haunted relic – squeaking and rustling wildlife.

I walked round the tank as far as I could, but its right side was completely tangled in brambles, and it would have taken a sharp machete and three native bearers to go round and take a good look at that. I satisfied myself with the left side and the back. I was interested to see that even the air vents for the engine had been welded up tight, and so had the grille over the driver's porthole.

Slinging my tape recorder over my shoulder, I heaved myself up on to the tank's mudguard. I made a lot of noise doing it, but I didn't suppose that thirty-year-old ghosts really objected that much to being disturbed in the night. Carefully, I walked across the blackened hull, and my footsteps sounded booming and metallic. I reached the turret, and hammered on it with my fist. It sounded very empty in there. I hoped it was.

As Jacques Passerelle had said, the tank's hatch was welded shut. It was a hasty-looking weld, but whoever had done it had known his job. As I strained forward to look at it more closely, however, I saw that the hatch was sealed by other means as well – means that, in their own way, were just as powerful.

Riveted over the top of the tank was a crucifix. It looked as if it had been taken from the altar of a church and crudely fastened to the turret in such a way that nobody could ever remove it. Looking even nearer, I saw that there was some kind of holy adjuration, too, engraved in the rough metal. Most of the words were corroded beyond legibility, but I could distinctly make out the phrase '*Thou art commanded to go out.*'

Up there on the hull of that silent ruined tank, in the dead of winter in Normandy, I felt frightened of the unknown for the first time in my life. I mean, really frightened. Even though I didn't want it to, my scalp kept chilling and prickling, and I found I was licking my lips again and again like a man in an icy desert. I could see the Citroën across the road, but the moon was reflecting from the flat windshield, so I couldn't make out Madeleine at all. For all I knew, she might have vanished. For all I knew, the whole of the rest of the world might have vanished. I coughed in the bitter cold.

I walked along to the front of the tank, pushing aside wild brambles and leafless creeper. There wasn't much to see there, so I walked back again to the turret, to see if I could distinguish more of the words.

It was then, as my fingers touched the top of the turret, that I heard someone laughing. I stayed stock still, holding my breath. The laughter stopped. I lifted my head, and tried to work out where the sound might have come from. It had been a short, ironic laugh, but with a peculiarly metallic quality, as if someone had been laughing over a microphone.

I said: 'Who's there?' but there was silence. The night was so quiet that I could still hear that distant dog barking. I laid my tape-recorder on top of the turret and clicked it on.

For several minutes, there was nothing but the hiss of the tape coursing past the recording head, and that damned dog. But then I heard a whispering sound, as if someone was talking to himself under his breath. It was close, and yet it seemed far away at the same time. *It was coming from the turret.*

Shaking and sweating, I knelt down beside the turret and tapped on it, twice. I sounded as choked up as a grade school kid after his first dry martini. I said: 'Who's there? Is there anybody inside there?'

There was a pause, and then I heard a whispery voice say: *'You can help me, you know.'*

It was a strange voice, which seemed to come from everywhere at once. It seemed to have a smile in it as well; the kind of voice that someone has when they're secretly grinning. It could have been a man or a woman or even a child, but I wasn't sure.

I said, 'Are you in there? Are you inside the tank?'

The voice whispered, *'You sound like a good man. A good man and true.'*

Almost screaming, I said: 'What are you doing in there? How did you get in?'

The voice didn't answer my question. It simply said, *'You can help me, you know. You can open this prison. You can take me to join my brethren. You sound like a good man and true.'*

'Listen!' I shouted. 'If you're really inside there, tap on the turret! Let me hear that you're in there!'

The voice laughed. *'I can do better than that. Believe me, I can do far better than that.'*

'I don't understand.'

34

The voice laughed softly. '*Do you feel sick?*' it asked me. '*Do you feel as if you're seized with cramps and pain?*'

I frowned. I did, as a matter of fact, feel nauseous. There was something in my stomach that was turning over and over; something foul and indigestible. I thought for a moment that it was something I ate for lunch; but then I was seized by a stomach spasm that made me realise I was going to be violently ill. It all happened in an instant. The next thing I knew, my gut was racked by the most terrible heaving, and my mouth had to stretch open wide as a torrent of revolting slush gushed out of me and splattered the hull of the tank. The vomiting went on and on until I was clutching my stomach and weeping from the sheer exhaustion of it.

Only then did I look at what had made me puke. Out of my stomach, out of my actual mouth, had poured thousands of pale twitching maggots, in a tide of bile. They squirmed and writhed all over the top of the tank, pink and half-transparent, and all I could do was clamber desperately off that hideous ruined Sherman and drop to the frozen grass, panting with pain and revulsion, and scared out of my mind.

Behind me, the voice whispered: '*You can help me, you know. You sound like a good man and true.*'

CHAPTER TWO

Father Anton carefully poured me a glass of Malmsey and brought it across his study at arm's length, as if it was a medical specimen. I took it unsteadily, and said, 'Thank you, father. That's very kind.'

He waved his hand as if to say not at all, not at all; and then sat his baggy ancient body in an armchair opposite, and opened up his snuff box.

'So you went to hear the voices,' he said, taking a pinch of ground tobacco.

I nodded.

'You look, forgive me for saying so, as if they alarmed you.'

'Not them. It.'

Father Anton snorted, sneezed, and blew his nose like the Trump of Doom. Then he said: 'Demons can be either. One demon can be *them*, or *it*, or whatever they please. A demon is a host of evils.'

I reached across to the small cherrywood sidetable and picked up my tape-recorder. 'Whatever it is, father, it's here, on tape, and it's an *it*. One infernal *it*.'

'You recorded it? You mean, you did actually hear it?'

The old priest's expression, which had been one of patient but not altogether unkind indulgence, subtly darkened and changed. He knew the voice or voices were real, because he had been to the tank himself and heard them. But for me to come along and tell him that I'd heard them, too – a perfect stranger without any kind of religious knowledge at all – well, that obviously disturbed him. Priests, I guess, are used to demons. They work, after all, in the spiritual front line, and they expect to be tempted and harassed by demonic manifestations. But when those manifestations are so evil and so powerful that they make themselves felt in the world of ordinary men, when the bad vibes are picked up by farmers and cartographers, then I reckon that most priests get to panic.

'I didn't come around last night because I was too sick,' I told Father Anton. 'I wanted to, but I couldn't.'

'The tank brought on your sickness? Is that it?'

I nodded, and my throat still tightened at the thought of what had poured out of my mouth.

'Whatever it is inside that tank, it made me vomit worms and bile. It took me half a dozen whiskys and a handful of paracetamol to get me over it.'

Father Anton touched the ecclesiastical ring on his finger. 'You were alone?' he asked me quietly.

'I went with Madeleine Passerelle. The daughter of Jacques Passerelle.'

Father Anton said gravely: 'Yes. I know that the Passerelles have been troubled by the tank for a long time.'

'Unfortunately, Madeleine didn't hear the voice first-hand. She stayed in the car because it was cold. But she's heard the recording, and she saw for herself how sick I was. The Passerelles let me stay the night at the farm.'

Father Anton indicated the tape-recorder. 'You're going to play it for me?'

'If you want to listen.'

Father Anton regarded me with a soft, almost sad look on his face. 'It has been a long time, *monsieur*, since anyone has come to me for help and guidance as you have. In my day, I was an exorcist and something of a specialist in demons and fallen angels. I will do everything I can to assist you. If what you have heard is a true demon, then we are facing great danger, because it is evidently powerful and vicious; but beguiling as well.'

He looked towards the empty fireplace. Outside, it

37

was snowing again, but Father Anton obviously believed it was more spiritual to sit in the freezing cold than to light a fire. I must say that I personally preferred to toast my feet and worry about the spirituality of it later.

Father Anton began. 'One thing I learned as an exorcist was that it is essential correctly to identify the demon with whom you are dealing. Some demons are easy to dispose of. You can say "The Father, the Son and the Holy Ghost, *boo*!" and they vanish back to hell. But others are more difficult. Adramelech, for instance, who is mentioned in the *Pseudomonarchia Daemonum*, which I have on the shelves right here. Or Belial. Then there is Beelzebub, Satan's successor, who was always notoriously difficult to banish. I never faced him myself, and it is probably best for me that I didn't. But I have an interesting account of how he possessed a nun at the Ursuline Convent at Aix-le-Provence in the seventeenth century, and how it took seven weeks of determined exorcism to dismiss him back to the netherworld.'

'Father Anton,' I said, as kindly as I could. 'This is all kind of medieval. I mean, what I'm trying to say is, we have something here that's evil, but it's modern.'

Father Anton smiled sadly. 'Evil is never modern, *monsieur*. It is only persistent.'

'But what happens if we have an ancient demon right here?'

'Well,' said the priest. 'Let us first hear the tape. Then perhaps we can judge who or what this voice might be. Perhaps it is Beelzebub himself, come to make a match of it.'

I wound back the cassette, pushed the 'play' button, and laid the tape-recorder on the table. There was a crackling sound; then the clank of metal as the tape-recorder was set down on the turret of the tank; then a short silence, interspersed with the barking of that distant dog. Father Anton leaned forward so that he could hear better, and cupped his hand around one ear.

'You realise that what you have here is very rare,' he told me. 'I have seen daguerrotypes and photographs of manifestations before, but never tape-recordings.'

The tape fizzed and whispered, and then that chilling, whispery voice said: *'You can help me, you know.'*

Father Anton stiffened, and stared across at me in undisguised shock.

The voice said: *'You sound like a good man. A good man and true. You can open this prison. You can take me to join my brethren. You sound like a good man and true.'*

Father Anton was about to say something, but I put my finger against my lips, warning him that there was more.

The voice went on: *'You can help me, you know. You and that priest. Look at him! Doesn't that priest have something to hide? Doesn't that priest have some secret lust, concealed under that holy cassock?'*

I stared at the tape-recorder in amazement. 'It didn't say that. There was no way it ever said that.'

Father Anton was white. He asked, in a trembling tone: 'What does this mean? What is it saying?'

'Father, father,' whispered the tape-recorder. *'Surely you recall the warm summer of 1928. So long ago, father, but so vivid. The day you took young Mathilde on the river, in your boat. Surely you remember that.'*

Father Anton rose jerkily to his feet, like a Victorian clockwork toy. His snuff tipped all over the rug. He stared at the tape-recorder as if it was the devil himself. His chest heaved with the effort of breathing, and he could scarcely speak.

'That day was innocent!' he breathed. 'Innocence itself! How dare you! How dare you suggest it was anything else! You! Demon! *Cochon! Vos mains sont sales avec le sang des innocents!*'

I reached out and seized Father Anton's sleeve. He tried to brush me away, but I gripped him more firmly, and said: 'Father, it's only a trick. For Christ's sake.'

Father Anton looked at me with watering eyes. 'A trick? I don't understand.'

'Father, it has to be. It's only a tape-recording. It's just some kind of trick.'

He looked nervously down at the cassette recorder, its tape still silently spinning. 'It can't be a trick,' he said huskily. 'How can a tape-recorder answer one back? It's not possible.'

'You heard it yourself,' I told him. 'It must be.'

I was as puzzled and scared as he was, but I didn't want to show it. I had the feeling that the moment I started giving in to all this weirdness, the moment I started believing it for real, I was going to get tangled up in something strange and uncontrollable. It was like standing at the entrance of a hall of mirrors, trying to resist the temptation to walk inside and find out what those distorted figures in the darkness were.

I pressed the tape-recorder's 'stop' button. The gloomy room was silent.

'Sit down, Father Anton,' I asked him. 'Now, let's play that tape back again, and we'll see how much of a trick it is.'

The old priest said: 'It's Satan's work. I have no doubt. It's the work of the devil himself.'

I gently helped him back to his armchair, and picked up his snuffbox for him. He sat there pale-faced and tense as I rewound the tape back to the beginning, and then pushed the 'play' button once again.

We waited tensely as the tape began to crackle and hiss. We heard it laid down on the turret again, and the dog barking. Then that voice began once more, and it seemed colder and even more evil than ever. It sounded as if it came from the throat of a hoarse hermaphrodite, some lewd creature who delighted in pain and pleasure and unspeakable acts.

'*You can help me, you know,*' it repeated. '*You sound like a good man. A good man and true. You can open this prison. You can take me to join my brethren. You sound like a good man and true.'*

Father Anton was sitting rigid in his seat, his knuckles spotted with white where he was clutching the frayed upholstery.

The voice said: *'Father Anton can take away the cross that binds me down, and cast away the spell. You can do that, can't you, Father Anton? You'd do anything for an old friend, and I'm an old friend of yours. You can take me to join my brethren across the waters, can't you? Beelzebub, Lucifer, Madilon, Solymo, Saroy, Theu, Ameclo, Sagrael, Praredun—'*

'Stop it!' shouted Father Anton. *'Stop it!'*

With unbelievable agility for a man as old as ninety, he reached out for the tape-recorder, held it in both hands, and smashed it against the steel fireguard around the grate. Then he sat back, his eyes staring and wild, snapping the broken pieces of plastic in his hands. He dragged out the thin brown tape, and crumpled it up into a confused tangle of knots and twists.

I sat watching all this in total amazement. First, I seemed to have a tape-recorder that said whatever it felt like. Now, I had a priest who broke up other people's property. I said: 'What's wrong? Why the hell did you do that?'

The priest took a deep breath. 'It was the conjuration,' he said. 'The words that can summon Beelzebub, the Lord of the Flies. There were only three more words to be said, and that demon could have been with us.'

'You're not serious.'

Father Anton held up the smashed fragments of Sony tape-recorder. 'Do you think I would break your machine for nothing? Those words can bring out of the under-world the most terrible of devils. I will buy you another, never fear.'

'Father Anton, it's not the tape-recorder I'm worried about. What concerns me is what goes *on* here. If there's a creature inside that tank, can't we do something about it? Exorcise it? Burn it out. Blow it up?'

Father Anton shook the smashed-up tape-recorder out of the skirts of his cassock and into the waste-paper basket. 'Exorcisms, my friend, are woefully misunderstood. They are hardly ever performed these days, and only in very serious cases of possession. As for burning the tank, or blowing it up, that would do no good. The demon would still haunt Pont D'Ouilly, although he would be more like a fierce dog on a long leash instead of a fierce dog inside a locked kennel. He cannot finally get away until the holy cross is lifted from the turret, and the words of dismissal erased.'

I opened the cigarette box on the table and took out a Gauloise. I lit it up and took a long drag. I was getting used to this pungent French tobacco, and if it didn't have as much tar in it as a three-mile stretch of the Allegheny Valley Expressway, I think I could have smoked it all the time. I said: 'Whatever it is, it obviously wants out.'

'Of course,' agreed Father Anton. 'And it appears to have a strong desire to rejoin its fellows. Its brethren. Perhaps it means that there were demons or devils possessing the other twelve tanks.'

'You mean *all* of them were possessed?'

'It seems likely. Why were they all painted black? Why were they all sealed down? You have said yourself that the Germans felt as if the devil was on their heels. I don't know whether you have yet had time to read your friend's history of the war, but the Orne Valley was taken at record speed – far more quickly than any of the surrounding countryside. Caen was shelled flat. But here – the tanks came through at top speed, and nobody short of Our Lord Himself could have stopped them.'

I blew out smoke. 'What you're suggesting is that this special division was made up of demons? I don't see now that's possible. Demons are – well, dammit, they're *demons*. They're medieval. They're imaginary. They don't fight wars.'

'On the contrary,' said Father Anton. 'That's precisely what they *do* do.'

'But how come nobody ever heard of this special division before? How come the Army even allowed it to happen? That's supposing it *did* happen, and all this isn't some kind of hoax.'

'Much that happened in the war is still secret. And, anyway, what were thirteen tanks among hundreds? Perhaps your government decided on a little experiment with black magic.'

'Father Anton, this doesn't seem real. If there's one thing that the Pentagon is not involved in, it's black magic!'

Father Anton went across to the tall window and looked down on his courtyard. Although it was mid-morning, it was as dark as late afternoon, and a few flakes of snow were tumbling idly across the village. The church clock struck eleven.

'What people forget,' he said, 'was that the war was mystic and magical in the extreme. Hitler set great store by magic, and made a particular point of confiscating the Spear of Longinus, the very spear that pierced Christ's side on the cross, from the Hofburg Museum in Vienna, because he believed that whoever possessed it could control the destiny of the world. On the side of the Allies, many experiments were made in sending messages by telepathy, and in levitation, and there was a Dutch priest who claimed he could invoke the wrath of the ten divine Sephiroth to bring down German planes with bolts of fire.'

I listened to this patiently, but I felt weary and sick. I said: 'Father, this is all very well, but what are we going to do about the tank?'

Father Anton turned towards me. 'There is nothing

43

we can do, *monsieur*. Wiser men than us have sealed that evil entity away, and it would be foolish to disturb it. If the authorities will not remove the tank, then it will have to stay there.'

'And the Passerelles will have to suffer the consequences for the rest of their lives? You know that Madeleine believes the tank killed her mother?'

The old priest nodded. 'She didn't tell me, but I guessèd as much. I wish there was more that I could do. All I can say is that I am very thankful we were left with only one tank, instead of many.'

I took a last hot drag of my Gauloise, and stubbed it out. 'Well, I think you're being too cautious,' I told him. 'Maybe it's time that someone gave the Passerelles a break, and maybe it's time the Pentagon got their dirty washing back.'

Father Anton looked at me and crossed himself. 'I can only warn you, *monsieur*, that to open the tank would be more than foolish. It would be tantamount to suicide.'

I stood up, and brushed ash off my pants. 'The taperecorder was 189 francs,' I said. 'But I'd be more than happy with half of that. It *was* kind of a joint venture, after all.'

Father Anton slowly shook his head. 'Perhaps one day I will understand Americans,' he said. 'And perhaps one day they will understand themselves.'

I met Madeleine for a glass of wine at lunchtime, in a small smokey café unappealingly called the Bar Touristique. A grossly fat woman in a floral housecoat served behind the bar, and occasionally forayed out to slap at the red formica-topped tables with a wet rag, as if they were disobedient dogs who kept playing up. The house wine was robust enough to clean your family silver with, but I'd managed to find a stale pack of Luckies in the local tobacconist's, so my palate wasn't complaining quite so vigorously as it had this morning.

Madeleine came in through the plastic-strip curtain looking very pale and waif-like, and when she saw me she came across the bar and put her arms tight around my neck.

'Dan, you're all right.'

'Of course I'm all right. I've only been talking to Father Anton.'

I took her speckled tweed coat and hung it up next to a sign that warned *Defense de Cracher*. She was wearing a plain turquoise-blue dress that was probably very fashionable in Pont D'Ouilly, but in Paris was about eight years out of style. Still, she looked good; and it was a lift to meet someone who really cared about my welfare. Ten-ton Tessie behind the bar brought us our wine, and we clinked glasses like one-time lovers meeting in a seedy bar at the back of Grand Central Station.

'Did you play Father Anton the tape?'

'Well, kind of.'

She touched my hand. 'There's something you don't want to tell me?'

'I don't know. I guess we're at a crossroads right now. We can either open the tank up, and find out what's in there, or we can forget it for ever, just like everyone else has.'

She reached up and stroked my cheek. Her pale eyes were full of concern and affection. If I hadn't been feeling so goddamned sick last night, lying doubled-up in the Passerelle's draughty spare bedroom, I think I might have tiptoed along the corridor and tapped on Madeleine's door, but I can tell you from first-hand experience that making love is the last thing you feel like after puking a mouthful of maggots; and I guess that even those who love you dearly find it kind of hard to give you a wholehearted kiss.

She sipped her wine. 'How can we leave it there?' she asked me. 'How can we just leave it there?'

'I don't know. But the mayor and the civic authorities

45

and even Father Anton himself seem to have managed to leave it there for thirty years.'

Madeleine said: 'You must think that I have a bee in my bonnet.'

'Where did they teach you to say that? The school of colloquial English?'

She looked up, and she wasn't smiling. 'The war was over years and years ago. Didn't we lose enough? Enough fathers and brothers and friends? They still sell postcards of Churchill and Eisenhower at the seaside resorts, and that makes me angry. They saved us, yes, but there is nothing glorious to celebrate. To fight wars is not glorious, not for anyone. It is better to forget. But, of course, they have left us their tank, and we can never forget.'

I sat back in my cheap varnished chair. 'So you want to open it up?'

Her eyes were cold. 'The thing itself said that it wanted to join its brethren. What can it want with us? If we let it out, it will go to meet its friends, and that will be the end of it.'

'Father Anton said that opening the tank would be as good as committing suicide.'

'Father Anton is old. And anyway, he believes that demons and devils have power over everything. He told me that once, in catechism class. "Madeleine," he said, "if it weren't for Jesus Christ, the whole world would be overrun with demons." '

I coughed. 'Supposing we open it up and there is a demon?'

She leaned forward intensely. 'There must be *something*, Dan. Otherwise we wouldn't have heard that voice. But demons don't have horns and forks. There's probably nothing inside there at all that the human eye can see.'

'Supposing there is?'

'That's what we have to find out.'

I drank some more wine, and I could almost feel it put hairs on my chest as I sat there. I said: 'What do they put in this stuff? Rust remover?'

Madeleine answered: 'Ssh. Madame Saurice used to entertain an American sergeant in the war, and she knows English well. All the slang English, like shucks.'

'*Shucks*? You sure it wasn't the war of 1812?'

Madeleine said, 'I never wanted to open the tank before, Dan. I never met anyone who gave me the strength to do it. My father wouldn't have touched it; nor would Eloise. But Eloise will tell us how to ward off demons and evil spirits while we do it, and I'm sure Father Anton will give you help if you ask him.'

I lit another cigarette. 'I don't see why it's so important to you. If you dislike the tank that much, why don't you move away? There isn't anything to keep you in Pont D'Ouilly, after all.'

'Dan, it's important because it lies on my father's farm, and my father's farm has always been home. Even if I go away for ever, that farm will still be the place where I was brought up, and that tank will still be there.'

She drank a little wine, and looked at me intently. 'And, anyway,' she said, 'I have dreamed about that tank ever since I was a little girl. That tank has given me terrible dreams.'

'Dreams? What kind of dreams?'

She lowered her eyes. 'They were cruel dreams. Nightmares. But they were exciting as well.'

'Sexually exciting?'

'Sometimes. I dreamed of being forced to have sex with bristly beasts and strange creatures. But sometimes the dreams were different, and I imagined that I was being mutilated or killed. That was frightening, but it was exciting, too. Pieces were being sliced off me, and there was lots of blood.'

I reached across the table and held her thin wrist.

'Madeleine . . . you know this tank isn't a joke. What's in there, whatever it is, is something really malign.'

She nodded. 'I have always known it. But I have also known, all my life, that one day I would have to face up to it. Of course, I tried to evade my responsibility. I tried to persuade you not to go down there to make your recording. But I am led to the conclusion that the time has probably come.'

'Well,' I said, 'it looks as though we've talked ourselves into it.'

She gave a fleeting, humourless smile.

Later that afternoon, I telephoned Father Anton and told him what we were planning to do. He was silent for a long time on the other end of the line, and then he said: 'I cannot persuade you otherwise?'

'Madeleine's set on it, and I guess I am, too.'

'You're not doing this out of a mistaken sense of affection for Madeleine? Because it can only do her harm, you know. You must realise that.'

I looked across the polished floor of Pont D'Ouilly's post office, marked with muddy footprints where the local farmers had come in to draw their savings or to post their letters. There was a tattered poster on the wall beside me warning of the dangers of rabies. Outside, a thin wet snow was falling, and the sky was unremittingly grey.

'It has to be done sometime, Father Anton. One day that tank's going to corrode right through, and that demon's going to get out anyway, and maybe someone completely unsuspecting is going to be passing by. At least *we* have some idea of what we're in for.'

Father Anton was silent for even longer. Then he said hoarsely: 'I'll have to come with you, you know. I'll have to be there. What time are you planning to do it?'

I glanced up at the post office clock. 'About three. Before it gets too dark.'

'Very well. Can you collect me in your car?'

'You bet. And thank you.'

Father Anton sounded solemn. 'Don't thank me, my friend. I am only coming because I feel it is my duty to protect you from whatever lies inside that tank. I would far rather that you left it alone.'

'I know that, father. But I don't think we can.'

He was waiting for me at the front door of his house, dressed in his wide black hat and black button-up boots, his cape as severe and dark as a raven. His housekeeper stood behind him and frowned at me disapprovingly, as if I was particularly selfish to take an old man out on an afternoon so cold and bleak; probably forgetting that it was colder inside his house than it was out. I helped him to climb into the front passenger seat, and smiled at the housekeeper as I walked around the car, but all she did was scowl at me from under her grubby lace cap, and slam the door.

As we drove off across the slushy grey cobbles of the priest's front courtyard, Father Anton said: 'Antoinette is what you probably call a fusspot. She believes she has divine instructions to make me wear my woollen underwear.'

'Well, I'm sure God cares about your underwear as much as He cares about anything else,' I told him, turning on the windshield wipers.

'My friend,' replied Father Anton, regarding me solemnly with his watery eyes, 'God will take care of the spirit and leave the underwear to look after itself.'

It took us about ten minutes to drive the back way around the village to the Passerelle's farm. The trees all around us were bare, and clotted with rooks' nests; and the fields were already hazy and white with snow. I beeped the Citroën's horn as we circled around the farmyard, and Madeleine came out of the door in a camel-hair duffel-coat, carrying an electric torch and an oily canvas bag full of tools.

I climbed out and helped her stow the kit away in the back of the car. She said: 'I got everything. The crowbars, the hammers. Everything you told me.'

'That's good. What did your father say?'

'He isn't so happy. But he says if we must do it, then we must. He's like everyone else. They would like to see the tank opened, but they are too frightened to do it themselves.'

I glanced at Father Anton, sitting patiently in his seat. 'I think that's how the good father feels about it. He's been dying to tackle this demon for years. It's a priest's job, after all. It just took a little coaxing.'

As I opened the door to let Madeleine into the back of the car, I heard Eloise calling from the kitchen. She came out into the dull afternoon, holding her black skirts up above the mud, and she was waving something in her hand.

'*Monsieur*! You must take this!'

She came nearer, and saw Father Anton sitting in the car, and nodded her head respectfully. 'Good day, father.'

Father Anton raised a hand in courteous greeting.

Eloise came up close to me and whispered: '*Monsieur*, you must take this. Father Anton may not approve, so don't let him see it. But it will help you against the creatures from hell.'

Into my hand, she pressed the same ring of hair that had been tied around the model cathedral in Jacques Passerelle's parlour. I held it up, and said, 'What is it? I don't understand.'

Eloise glanced at Father Anton apprehensively, but the old priest wasn't looking our way. 'It is the hair of a firstborn child who was sacrificed to Moloch centuries ago, when devils plagued the people of Rouen. It will show the monsters that you have already paid your respects to them.'

I said, 'I really don't think—'

Eloise clutched my hands in her own bony fingers. 'It doesn't matter what you think, *monsieur*. Just take it.'

I slipped the ring of hair into my coat pocket, and climbed into the car without saying anything else. Eloise watched me through the snow-streaked window as I started up the motor, and turned the car around. She was still standing on her own in the wintry farmyard as we drove out of the gates and splashed our way through the melting slush en route to Pont D'Ouilly itself, and the tank.

Twisted into the hedgerow, the tank was lightly dusted with snow, and it looked more abandoned than ever. But we all knew what was waiting inside it, and as we got out of the Citroën and collected together the torch and the tools, none of us could keep our eyes off it.

Father Anton walked across the road, and took a large silver crucifix from inside his coat. In his other hand, he held a Bible, and he began to say prayers in Latin and French as he stood in the sifting snowflakes, his wide hat already white, with the low cold wind blowing the tails of his cape.

He then recited the dismissal of demons, holding the crucifix aloft as he did so, and making endless invisible crosses in the air.

'I adjure thee, O vile spirit, to go out. God the Father, in His name, leave my presence. God the Son, in His name, make thy departure. God the Holy Ghost, in His name, quit this place. Tremble and flee, O impious one, for it is God who commands thee, for it is I who command thee. Yield to me, to my desire by Jesus of Nazareth who gave His soul. To my desire by sacred Virgin Mary who gave Her womb, by the blessed Angels from whom thou fell. I demand thee be on thy way. Adieu O spirit, Amen.'

We waited for a while, shivering in the cold, while

51

Father Anton stood with his head bowed. Then he turned to us, and said, 'You may begin.'

Hefting the canvas bag of tools, I climbed up on to the tank's hull. I reached back and helped Madeleine to scramble after me. Father Anton waited where he was, with the crucifix raised in one hand, and the Bible pressed to his breast.

I stepped carefully across to the turret. The maggots that I'd vomited yesterday had completely disappeared, as if they'd been nothing more than a rancid illusion. I knelt down and opened the canvas bag, and took out a long steel chisel and a mallet. Madeleine, kneeling beside me, said, 'We can still turn back.'

I looked at her for a moment, and then I reached forward and kissed her. 'If you have to face this demon, you have to face it. Even if we turn back today, we'll have to do it sometime.'

I turned to the tank's turret, and with five or six ringing blows, drove the edge of the chisel under the crucifix that was riveted on to the hatch. Thirty years of corrosion had weakened the bolts, and after five minutes of sweaty, noisy work, the cross was off. Then, just to make sure, I hammered the last few legible words of the holy adjuration into obscurity.

Breathing hard, I stood still for a while and listened. There was no sound except for my own panting, and the soft whispery fall of the snow. In the distance, it was almost impossible to see the trees and the farm rooftops any more, because the snow was thickening and closing in; but Father Anton stood alert with his white hat and white shoulders, still holding the silver crucifix up in his mittened hand.

I tapped on the turret, and said, 'Is anyone there? Is anyone inside?'

There was no answer. Just the dull echo of my cautious knock.

I wiped my chilled, perspiring forehead. Madeleine,

her hair crowned in snowflakes, tried to give me a confident smile.

'Well,' I said, 'this is the big one.'

With a wide steel chisel, I banged all the way round the hatch of the turret, breaking the rough welding wherever I could, but mostly knocking dents in the rusted armour plating. I was making my seventh circle of the hatch when the blade of the chisel went right through a deeply corroded part of the metal, and made a hole the size of a dime.

Even in the freezing cold, even in the blanketing snow, we heard the sour whistle of fetid air escaping from the inside of the tank, and a smell came out of that Sherman like I'd never smelled anywhere before. It had the stomach-turning sickliness of rotten food, mingled with an odour that reminded me of the reptile houses at zoos. I couldn't help retching, and Madame Saurice's rough red wine came swilling back up into my mouth. Madeleine turned away and said: '*Mon Dieu!*'

I tried to hold myself steady, and then I turned back to Father Anton and said, 'I've broken a hole through, father. It smells really disgusting in there.'

Father Anton crossed himself. 'It is the odour of Baal,' he said, his face grey in the afternoon cold. Then he raised the crucifix higher and said: 'I conjure bind and charge thee by Lucifer, Beelzebub, Sathanas, Jauconill and by their power, and by the homage thou owest unto them, that you do torment and punish this disobedient demon until you make him come corporally to my sight and obey my will and commandments in whatsoever I shall charge or command thee to do. Fiat, fiat, fiat. Amen.'

Madeleine whispered: 'Dan – we could seal it up again. There's still time.'

I looked at the tiny hole, out of which the polluted air still sang. 'And then how long before it gets out of here, and comes after us? This thing killed your mother,

Madeleine. If you really believe that, we have to get rid of it for good.'

'Do *you* believe it?' she asked me, her eyes wide.

'I don't know. I just want to find out what's inside here. I want to find out what it is that can make a man puke maggots.'

I licked my lips, and raised the hammer once again. Then I struck the turret again and again until the hole grew from a dime to a quarter, and eventually the armour plating began to break off in leaves of black rust. Within twenty minutes, I'd broken all the metal away around the hinges of the hatch, and the hole was the size of a large frying-pan.

Father Anton, still waiting patiently in the snow, said: 'Can you see anything, *monsieur*?'

I peered into the blackness of the tank's interior. 'Nothing so far.'

Taking a crowbar from the canvas bag, I climbed up on top of the Sherman's turret, and inserted one end of the crowbar into the hole. Then I leaned back, and slowly began to raise the hatch itself, like opening a stubborn can of tomatoes with a skewer. Eventually, the welding broke, and the hatch came free. I stood there breathless and hot, even in the sub-zero temperature of that gloomy afternoon, but at least the job was done. I said to Madeleine: 'Hand me the flashlight.'

Her face pale, she passed it over. I switched it on, and pointed the beam downwards into the Sherman's innards. I could see the tank commander's jumpseat, the breech of the cannon, and the gunlayer's seat. I flicked the beam sideways, and then I saw it. A black sack, dusty and mildewed, and sewn up like a mailbag, or a shroud. It wasn't very large – maybe the size of a child, or a bag of fertiliser. It was lying next to the side of the tank as if it had fallen there.

Madeleine touched my shoulder. 'What is it?' she whispered in a frightened voice. 'What can you see?'

I stood straight. 'I don't know. It's a kind of black bag. I think I'll have to go down there and lift it out.'

Father Anton called: '*Monsieur!* Don't go in there!'

I took another look at the bag. 'It's the only way. We'll never get it out of there otherwise.'

The last thing in the whole world I wanted to do was get down inside that tank and touch that bag, but I knew that if we tried to hook it out with the crowbar we'd probably tear the fabric. It looked pretty old and rotten – more than thirty years old, maybe more than a hundred. One rip and whatever was inside it was going o come spilling out.

While Madeleine held back the jagged hatch for me, ı carefully climbed up on to the turret and lowered my legs inside. Even though my feet were freezing cold, I had a strange tingling feeling, as if something inside the tank was going to bite them. I said hoarsely, 'I always wanted to see what a tank looked like inside,' and then I lowered myself into the chilled, musty interior.

Tanks are claustrophobic enough when they're heated and lighted and they're not possessed by aemonic sacks. But when I clambered down into that cramped and awkward space, with wheels and instruments hitting my head and shoulders, and only a flashlight for company, I felt a surge of fear and suffocation, and all I wanted to do was get out of there.

I took a deep breath. It still smelled pretty foul in there, but most of the odour had dispersed. I looked up and saw Madeleine's face at the open hatch. She said nervously, 'Have you touched it yet?'

I shone my torch on the sack. There was something or somebody inside it, whatever it was. As close as this, the fabric looked even older than I'd imagined. It could almost have been a piece of the Bayeux tapestry, or a medieval shroud.

I reached my hand out and touched it. The cloth was soft with age. I ran my fingers gently along the length of it, and I could feel various protrusions and sharp knobs. It felt like a sack of bones; an old and decaying sack of bones.

I coughed. I told Madeleine: 'I'm going to try and lift it up to you. Do you think you can take it?'

She nodded. 'Don't be long. Father Anton's looking very cold.'

'I'll try not to be.'

I wedged the flashlight against a hydraulic pipe so that it shone across the inside of the turret, and then I knelt down beside the sack. It took a lot of summoning-up of nerve, but in the end I put my arms around the black fusty cloth, and lifted it a foot or so upwards. It was saggy, and whatever was inside it, the bones or whatever they were, tumbled to one end of the sack with a soft rattling sound. But the fabric didn't tear, and I was able to gather the whole thing up in my arms and lift it towards Madeleine. She reached down and gripped the top of it, and I said: 'Okay, heave.'

For one moment, for one terrifying moment, just as Madeleine took the weight of the sack and hoisted it upwards, I was sure that I felt it wriggle, as if there was something alive inside it. It could have been a bone shifting, or my own keyed-up imagination, but I took my hands away from that sack as fast as if it was burning.

Madeleine gasped. 'What is it? What's happened?'

'Just get that sack out of here quick!' I yelled. '*Quick!*'

She tugged it upwards, and for a few seconds it snared on the rough metal around the broken-open hatch. But then she swung it clear, and I heard it drop on the hull outside. Taking the flashlight, I climbed out of the tank on to the turret, and I haven't ever been so glad to see snow and miserable gloomy skies as I was then.

Father Anton was approaching the side of the tank where the black sack lay. He was holding the crucifix and the Bible in front of him, and his eyes were fixed on our strange discovery like the eyes of a man who comes across the evidence, at last, that his wife has really been cuckolding him.

He said: '*Enfin, le diable.*'

I touched the sack tentatively with my foot. 'That was all there was. It feels like it's full of bones.'

Father Anton didn't take his eyes away from the sack for a second.

'Yes,' he said, 'the bones of a demon.'

I swung myself down from the hull of the tank, and helped Madeleine to jump down after me. 'I didn't know demons *had* bones,' I remarked. 'I thought they were all in the mind.'

'No, no,' said Father Anton. 'There was a time, in the Middle Ages, when demons and gargoyles walked the earth as living creatures. There is too much evidence to refute it. Paul Lucas, the medieval traveller, tells how he actually met the demon Asmodeus in Egypt, and the demon Sammael was said to have walked through the streets of Rouen as late as the twelfth century.'

Madeleine said: 'We don't yet know that it's really bones. It could be anything.'

Father Anton returned his Bible to his pocket. 'Of course, of course. We can take it back to my house. I have a cellar where we can lock it up safely. It seems to be acquiescent enough now.'

I looked at Madeleine, but she simply shrugged. If the priest wanted to take the sack back home with him, then there wasn't much we could do to stop him. I just hoped that the thing wouldn't decide to wake up and take its revenge on any of us for being disturbed so unceremoniously on a cold December afternoon.

I opened the back of the Citroën, and between us we carried the sagging, musty sack across the road and laid it gently in the car. Then I collected up the tools that Madeleine's father had lent us, and climbed into the car myself. Father Anton, taking off his hat and shaking the snow off it, said: 'I feel strangely elated. Can you understand that?'

I started the motor. 'This is what you've wanted to do for thirty years, isn't it? Open the tank and find out what the hell's happening.'

'Mr McCook,' he said, 'you should have come here years ago. It takes unusual simplicity, unusual directness, to do something like this.'

'I'm not sure whether that's a compliment or not.'

'I didn't mean naïveté.'

We drove through the gathering dusk, and the thick snowflakes whirled and tumbled all around us. But the time we reached Father Anton's house in the middle of the village, the church clock was striking five, and we could hardly see through the pouring snow. The housekeeper opened the door as we arrived, and stood there with a sour face and her hands clasped across her apron as I helped Father Anton into the porch.

'*Il a quatre-vingt-dix ans,*' she snapped, taking the old man's arm and leading him inside. '*Et il faut sortir dans la neige pour jouer comme un petit garçon?*'

'Antoinette,' said Father Anton reassuringly, patting her hand. 'I have never felt so healthy.'

Madeleine and I went round to the back of the Citroën, and lifted out the sack. From the dark hall, Father Anton called: 'That's right, bring it inside. Antoinette – will you bring me the keys to the cellar?'

Antoinette stared suspiciously at the black bundle we were carrying through the snow.

'*Qu'est-ce que c'est?*' she demanded.

'*C'est un sac de charbon,*' smiled Father Anton.

With one last backward look of ultimate distrust, Antoinette went off to fetch the cellar keys, while Madeleine and I laid our unholy bundle down in the hall.

Father Anton said: 'If these *are* bones, then I have a ceremony for disposing of them. The bones of a demon are just as potent as the live demon itself, so the books

58

say; but they can be scattered in such a way that the demon cannot live again. The skull has to be interred in one cathedral, and the hands and the feet in three others. Then the remaining bones are laid to rest in churches all around the intervening countryside, in ritual sequence.'

I took out my handkerchief and blew my nose. It was so cold that I could hardly feel it. 'Supposing we ask the Pentagon how to get rid of it?' I asked. 'After all, they put it there in the first place.'

Father Anton looked down at the black sack and shook his head. 'I don't know. I think the most important thing is to exorcise this beast as quickly as possible.'

Antoinette came bustling back with the cellar keys, and handed them to Father Anton. She pursed her lips in disapproval, but then Father Anton said gently, 'I would love some of your barley broth, Antoinette,' and she softened a little, and went off to the kitchen to prepare it.

Madeleine and I lifted the soft, yielding sack once more, and Father Anton said; 'Follow me.' But as we shuffled off down the long polished hallway, I glanced back at the place where the sack had been lying, and a feeling went down my shoulders like ice sliding down the inside of my shirt.

The wooden floor had been burned, as if by a poker. Where the black sack had been laid, there was the distinct, unmistakable outline of a small, hunched skeleton.

'Father Anton,' I whispered.

The old priest turned and saw the burns. He said: 'Lay down the sack, gently.' Then while we settled the decaying black fabric on the floor again, he walked back on creaking boots and knelt stiffly and painfully down His fingers traced the pattern that was scorched into the woodblock flooring, touching it as respectfully and gently as a fine medieval brass. I stood behind him and said 'Do you know what it is?'

He didn't look up. 'Oh, yes,' he said quietly. 'I know what it is. It is the mark of the demon. This house is holy, you see. It has been the vessel of years of prayer and blessings. And a demon's bones cannot touch it without making a mark.'

'It looks very small. Not much more than a child.'

'It is no smaller than the devils and gargoyles that are carved on medieval churches, my friend. We forget that many of those were carved, secretly, from the actual bodies of such fiends. I have the memoirs upstairs of a stonemason who worked at Chartres, and he tells of how the monks would bring him skulls and bones of creatures that he could never identify.'

Madeleine came up and took my arm. 'What are we going to do?' she asked softly. 'What if it tries to break free?'

'We must take it to the cellar at once,' said Father Anton. 'I can confine it there by the power of the crucifix and the power invested in me by Our Lord Jesus Christ. Then, at the first opportunity, we must take the skeleton to pieces and scatter those pieces according to the *Sepher Ha Zohar*, which is the most important book of the Kabbalah.'

We returned to the black sack, and this time all three of us took hold of it, and we walked with it as quickly as we could to the carved oak door of the cellar, way down at the end of the hall. Once we were there, Father Anton took out the largest of his keys, and put it into the lock.

Inside the door, it smelled of limestone and must. Father Anton switched on the light, and said, 'Be careful of the stairs. They're very old and uneven.'

Like the cellars of most French houses of any size, Father Anton's was enormous, and divided into several rooms. I could see wine racks through one half-open door, and inside another, garden tools and pieces of medieval masonry. But Father Anton directed us down to the very farthest recesses of the cellar, to a heavy door studded with black iron nails, and opened it up with another elaborate key.

This room was totally dark inside, and airless. There were no windows, and the room was empty but for a few broken flowerpots and a rusted mangle. It was floored with dusty clay tiles, and whitewashed with lime. Father Anton switched on the single bare bulb and said: 'Lay the sack down here. This room was originally used for storing valuables and furniture. The lock is very strong.'

We set the black bag down in the centre of the room, and stood back from it with considerable relief. Father Anton reached inside his coat and took out his worn brown spectacle case.

'First of all, we have to find out what kind of a demon this is,' he said. 'Then we can do our best to dismiss it. Mr McCook – you'll find a garden sickle in the next room. Perhaps you'd be kind enough to bring it in.'

I went to fetch the sickle while Father Anton stalked impatiently around the flaccid, lumpy bag, staring at it closely through his gold-rimmed spectacles, and coughing from time to time in the cold air of the cellar.

There were five sickles of varying sizes, so being a native of Mississippi I chose the largest. I took it back to Father Anton, and he smiled, and said, 'Will *you* cut it open? Or shall I?'

I looked across at Madeleine. She was tired and tense, but she obviously wanted to know what horrors were contained inside this sack just as much as I did. She nodded, and I said, 'Okay – I'll do it.'

I leaned over the sack and pushed the point of the sickle into the ancient fabric. It went in easily, and when I tugged, the bag ripped softly open with a dusty, purring sound, as fibre parted from fibre after centuries of waiting for unimaginable reasons in places that could only be guessed at.

61

The bag was full of dust and bones. I stood back, and stared at the bones with a kind of horrified curiosity, because they weren't the bones of any human or beast that you'd recognise. There were narrow ribs, curved thighbones, long claw-like metatarsals. They were dull brown and porous, and they looked as if they were six or seven hundred years old, or even more. I'd once dug up the skeleton of a Red Indian at my father's place at Louin, in Jasper County, and that had the same dry look about it.

It wasn't the bones of the body that frightened me so much; though they were grotesque enough in themselves. It was the skull. It had its jawbone missing, but it was a curious beaklike skull, with slanting eye-sockets, and a row of small nib-like teeth. There were rudimentary horns at the back of the head, and if it hadn't have been for the reptilian upper jaw, I would have said it was the skull of a goat.

Madeleine took my hand, and squeezed it hard. 'What is it?' she said, in a voice unsteady with fear. 'Dan – *what is it?*'

Father Anton took off his spectacles, and closed them with a quiet click. He looked at us, and his eyes were red from tiredness and cold, but his face was alive with human compassion and religious fortitude. He had been a priest for seventy years, twice as long as either of us had been alive, and even though he was elderly, he had seen in those seventy years enough miracles and enough demonic fears to give him strength where we had very little.

He said, 'It is just as I suspected.

I raised an eyebrow. 'You suspected something? You mean, you *guessed* what this was beforehand?'

He nodded. 'It was after we spoke, after we talked about the thirteen tanks. I spent an hour or so looking through the *Pseudomonarchia Daemonum*, and I came across a small reference to *les treize diables de Rouen*. There is very little there, very little information. But it appears from what Jean Wier says that in 1045 the city of Rouen was terrorised by thirteen devils which brought fire, pestilence, sorrow, and disaster. They were the thirteen acolytes of Adramelech, who was the eighth demon in the hierarchy of the evil Sephiroth, and the grand Chancellor of Hell.'

I reached inside my coat for my stale Lucky Strikes. I said, 'Is it that unusual to find devils in teams of thirteen?'

'Well, quite.'

'But what were thirteen eleventh-century devils doing in thirteen American tanks in the Second World War? It doesn't make any sense.'

Father Anton shrugged. 'I don't know, Mr McCook. Perhaps if we knew the answer to that, we would know the answer to everything.'

Madeleine asked: 'What happened to the devils of Rouen? Does the book say?'

'Oh, yes. They were imprisoned in a dungeon by a powerful spell imposed on them by the medieval exorcist Cornelius Prelati. The book is in medieval French, so it's a little difficult to decipher exactly how, or for how long. But it mentioned the word *coud^e*, which I thought at first meant that the devils were imprisoned very close together, rubbing shoulders. However, when I saw this sack I realised that there could be some connection. The French word *coudre*, as you may know, *monsieur*, means "to sew up." '

Madeleine whispered, 'The devils were sewn in bags. Just like this one.'

Father Anton said nothing, but raised his hands as if to say, *c'est possible*.

We stood around the bones for a long time in silence. Then Madeleine said: 'Well, what's to be done?'

Father Anton sucked at his ill-fitting dentures. 'We must spread the bones across the countryside, as the

63

Kabbalah recommends. But of course we cannot do it tonight. In any event, I shall have to call every one of the church authorities involved, and ask for permission to bury the bones in such a way.'

'That's going to take forever,' I told him.

Father Anton nodded. 'I know. But I'm afraid that it's necessary. I cannot simply bury the bones of a creature like this on sacred ground without the knowledge of the church.'

Madeleine took my hand. Very naturally, very easily, and very affectionately. She said, 'Dan, perhaps you ought to stay with Father Anton tonight. I don't like to leave him alone with this thing.'

Father Anton smiled. 'It is kind of you to feel such concern. But you really needn't worry.'

'No, no,' I told him. 'I'd like to. That's if you don't mind.'

'Of course not. We can have a game of chess together after dinner.'

I said to Madeleine, 'I'll run you home.'

Father Anton switched off the light in the room where the demon's remains lay scattered. For a moment we paused at the door, looking back into the pitch darkness. I could have sworn I felt a light breeze, sour with the same odour that had pervaded the tank, coursing out of the room. Of course, it was impossible. The room had no windows. But all the same, there was this strange, unsettling sensation, as if you were awakened in the night by the breath from some creature's nostrils on your cheek.

Father Anton closed the heavy door and locked it. Then he stood before it, and crossed himself, and spoke a prayer I'd never heard in my whole life.

'O devil,' he whispered, 'thou who hast touched no food, drunk no water, tasted not the sprinkled flour nor known the sacred wine, remain within I command thee. O gate, do not open that the demon within may pass; O lock hold thyself firm; O threshold stay untrod. For the day of the Lord is at hand, when the dead shall rise and outnumber the living, in His name's sake, amen.'

The old priest crossed himself again, and so did Madeleine. I wished right then that I'd had that kind of religion, too – the kind of religion that gave me words and actions to guard me against the devils of the night.

'Come,' said Father Anton. 'Perhaps you'd like a calvados before you take Mademoiselle Passerelle home.'

'I think I could use it,' I told him, and we went upstairs, with only one backward glance at the door that held back the bones of the demon.

After drinks and cakes, I drove Madeleine home through the streets of Pont D'Ouilly to her father's farm. The snow had eased up, and now the Orne Valley was silent and cold and the hills surrounding the river were as white as furniture covered in dust-sheets. There was a pale moon rising, weaker than last night, and the snow-grey fields were patterned with the footprints of birds and stoats.

I stopped the car at the gate. Madeleine buttoned up her coat and said, 'You won't come in?'

'Maybe tomorrow. I promised Father Anton a game of chess. I think he's deserved it.'

She nodded, and reached out for my hand. 'I don't know how to thank either of you. It's like a great weight that's been taken off my family's shoulders.'

I rubbed my eyes. I was feeling the strain of what we had done this afternoon, both mentally and physically. My arms were aching from all that chiselling and hammering, and my mind was still a little tender from those claustrophobic moments inside the tank. I said, 'Thank me tomorrow, when I can work out why the hell I wanted to do it in the first place.'

She smiled. 'I thought Americans were just naturally helpful.'

'More like naturally nosey!'

She leaned across the car, which wasn't difficult, because the 2CV's so tiny that you're sitting pressed together like canned frankfurters in any case. Her lips touched my cheek, and then we kissed, and I suddenly discovered that Norman farm girls have a really good flavour that almost makes demon-hunting worthwhile.

I said quietly, 'I thought French people kissed each other on the cheeks.'

She looked at me closely, and said: 'That's only when they're handing out medals.'

'Isn't that what you're doing now?'

She didn't answer for a long time, but then she said: *'Peut-être, monsieur. Qui sait?'*

She opened her door and climbed out into the snow. She stayed where she was for a while, looking up and down the white and silent road, and then she leaned into the car and said, 'Will I see you tomorrow?'

'Sure. Why don't you come up to Father Anton's sometime during the morning? I guess we have a lot of phoning to do. Calling up all those priests and getting rid of all those bones.'

Her breath smoked in the reflected light from the Citroën's headlights. She said, 'Sleep well, Dan. And, again – thank you.'

Then she shut the car door, and walked through the snow-topped gate-posts into her father's farmyard. I watched her for a while, but she didn't turn round, so I backed up the car and drove off towards Pont D'Ouilly, with only a quick sideways glance at the hulk of the Sherman tank which now rested in the hedge like the black discarded chrysalis of some monstrous insect.

The library, with its rows of leather books and its dismal portraits, was chillingly cold; so while we played chess after dinner, Father Anton allowed us the extravagance of two large elm logs on the fire, and we sat with glasses of Napoleon brandy beside the flickering flames, talking and playing slow, elaborate games until almost midnight.

'You play quite well,' observed Father Anton, after checkmating my king for the third straight time. 'You're out of practice, though, and you're too impatient. Before you move, think – and then think again.'

'I'm trying to. I guess I have other things on my mind.'

'Like our demon? You mustn't.'

'It's kind of hard to forget.'

Father Anton took a pinch of snuff and poked it ceremoniously up his left nostril. 'The devil thrives on fear, my friend. The more you fear him, the fiercer he becomes. You must think of what we have downstairs in the cellar as nothing more than a heap of stray bones, such as any hound might have buried in the cabbage-patch.'

'Well, I'll try.'

Father Anton moved his pawn to rook six, and then sat back in his studded leather armchair. While I frowned at the chessboard and tried to work my way out of a situation that, on the face of it, looked like a fourth checkmate in three moves, he sipped his brandy ruminatively, and said, 'Does it surprise you that demons actually lived? That they had flesh, and bones?'

I looked up. He was staring at the fire, and the flames reflected from his spectacles.

I said, 'I don't know. I suppose it does. I wouldn't have believed it unless I'd seen it for myself.'

Father Anton shrugged. 'It seems strange to me, you know, that in an age as pragmatic as ours, an age so bent on seeking evidence and demonstration, that the tangible manifestations of religion, like demons and devils, should be scoffed at.'

'Come on! Not many people have ever seen a demon.'

Father Anton turned his head and looked at me

67

seriously. 'Haven't they? They'd be surprised. Demons and devils have evolved like the rest of us, and it's remarkable how many of them still hide on the face of the earth.'

'Does the same go for angels?' I asked him. 'I mean – do we have anyone on our side?'

Father Anton shook his head. 'Angels never existed as actual creatures. The name "angel" describes a state of divine energy that is terrible in the classic sense of the word. I know that angels are the messengers of God; and that they often protect us from harm and from the temptations of Satan. But I know enough about them to say that, in this life, I would prefer not to meet one. They are fearsome to say the least.'

'Can they be summoned, like demons?'

'Not in the same way. But if you're interested, I have a book on my shelves on the invocation of angels. It was a great favourite of the Reverend Taylor when he was here during the war, surprisingly. Perhaps his involvement with your country's demons alarmed him sufficiently to seek some assistance from the cohorts of God.'

We fell silent for a few minutes while I made my next move on the board. Outside the tall windows, the snow began to fall again, thick and silent, piling softly on to northern France until it looked like the moon. An easterly wind was blowing across Poland and Germany and Belgium, bringing low clouds and an endless winter of grey cold.

Father Anton inspected the chessboard. '*Ce n'est pas mal, ça,*' he said, nodding his head in approval. But then his bony, liver-spotted hand moved his queen across towards my king, and he said: '*Malheureusement, c'est éche et mat.*'

With one move, he had stymied my king; and all I could do was lift my hands in surrender. 'I guess I had to learn the hard way. Never play chess with nonagenarians.'

He smiled. 'We must play some more, if you're staying in the Suisse Normande. You're a worthy opponent.'

'Thanks,' I said, lighting a cigarette. 'But I'm afraid that baseball's more my style.'

We finished our brandy as the carved mahogany clock on the mantelpiece struck twelve. The logs in the grate sparked and dropped, and all around us was the silence of a dark clerical mansion in the heart of a small wintry village in the shouldering hills of Normandy. Father Anton spoke. 'This is a brave thing you have done today. You must realise that. I know that Madeleine is appreciative, but I am, too. I'm very sad that, for all these years, there hasn't been a man among us with sufficient courage to do what you did, and open the tank up.'

'You know what they say,' I told him. 'Ignorance is bliss. If I'd known as much as you do about devils and demons, I probably wouldn't have gone near it.'

'Nonetheless, *monsieur*, I am grateful. And I want you to wear this tonight, my crucifix, as a protection.'

He lifted the large silver cross from around his neck and passed it over. It was weighty, and embossed with the figure of Christ. I held it in my hand for a moment, and then I offered it back to him. 'I can't wear this. This is yours. You need protection as much as I do.'

Father Anton smiled. 'No, *monsieur*. I have my wits and my training to protect me, and above all I have my God.'

'You don't think that it – well, might attack us?'

The old priest shrugged. 'You can never tell with devils. I don't yet know which devil this is, although we've guessed it might be one of the thirteen demons of Rouen. It might be powerful, it might be weak. It might be treacherous or wrathful. Until we have done the seven tests on it, we shall not be able to find out.'

'The seven tests?'

'Seven ancient tests which identify whether a devil is

of hell or of earth; whether it spreads its evil by pestilence or by fire; whether it is high in the ranks of the evil Sephiroth, or whether it is nothing more than a servile thing that creeps upon the face of the earth.'

I rose from my chair and walked across the room. Outside, the snow tumbled and twisted through the night, and the front of Father Anton's house was like a pale execution yard, untrod, unmarked with blood.

'Are you frightened?' Father Anton said, in a husky voice.

I paused for a moment to think. Then I said: 'Yes, I think so.'

'Then kneel here, *monsieur*, if you will; and I shall say a prayer for you.'

I turned round. He was sitting by the dying fire with a look of real concern on his face. I said gently: 'No thank you, father. Tonight I think I'll trust to luck.'

CHAPTER THREE

I was to sleep in a high green-painted iron bed in a small room on the uppermost floor. Father Anton lent me a voluminous white nightshirt, white bed-socks, and a copy of *L'Invocation des Anges*, leather-bound and smelling of dust, to read by the light of my shaky bedside lamp.

We said goodnight on the second floor, where Father Anton himself slept, and then I creaked up through the gloomy house to the long narrow corridor where my own room was. Antoinette had left the light on upstairs, despite Father Anton's usual frugality, and I was grateful for it. I beetled along that corridor as if the ten evil Sephiroth were panting down my neck, closed my door and locked it.

The room was plain, but it wasn't bad. Apart from the bed, there was a cheap pine dresser with a mirror, and one of those vast French wardrobes in which to hang my crumpled coat and shirt. There was a washbasin in one corner, and a circular window with a view over the snowy rooftops of Pont D'Ouilly. I washed with hard kitchen soap, rinsed my mouth out with water, and then pulled on Father Anton's nightshirt. I looked like Stan Laurel in one of those movies where Laurel and Hardy have to spend the night in a haunted house.

The springs complained noisily when I climbed into bed. I sat upright for a while, listening to the sounds of the house and the night outside; and then I opened the book that Father Anton had lent me, and started to read.

My French was so halting that it took me half an hour to read the first page, and that was a lengthy apology from the author, Henri St Ermin, for his platitudinous style and his lack of talent with a pen. I couldn't have agreed with him more. I skipped the text and looked at the engravings instead.

I began to understand what Father Anton had meant when he said that angels were terrible. There were drawings of angels that were nothing but intense sources of light with spreading wings. There were angels like fierce, proud beasts. And there were angels who were unseen, but who came at night like violent storms, and laid waste to the houses of the wicked. It was plain from the captions under each of the pictures that you had to invoke the right angel for the right temporal task, otherwise you might find yourself, metaphorically speaking, plugging a flashlight bulb into a nuclear power station. One caption warned of 'the angel which comes in a cloak of clouds, in which are the faces of those who have sinned and repented their sins'.

Outside in the snow, the church clock struck two, and I closed my less-than-reassuring midnight reader, switched off my light, and settled down to get some sleep. In the dark, the house seemed even noisier than it had with the lights on. Something scurried and flurried up in the attic above me, and the joists and timbers creaked and groaned and complained to each other like arthritic old women in a doctor's waiting-room.

I slept for maybe ten minutes; and woke to hear my watch ticking on the bedside table. The house was quieter now, and I fell asleep again, although this time I began to dream. I dreamed I was opening doors in a gloomy building, and behind each door there was something fearful. I could hardly bear to place my hand on the doorknobs and turn them, but I had a terrible compulsion to find out what was there. Through the tenth or the eleventh door, there was a narrow corridor, and at the end of the corridor someone was standing. Someone small, like a child, with its back to me. I began to work my way slowly and glutinously down the corridor to see who it was, and all the time I knew that it was someone frightening, but all the time I was compelled to find out, compelled to go on.

As I came close, the small figure turned towards me, and for one moment I saw a face that grinned like a goat, with hideous yellow eyes. I was so scared that I woke up, and I was sitting upright in bed with my nightshirt tangled around my legs, sweating and chilled, and this time the church clock was just pealing three.

I switched on my bedside light and swung out of bed. I listened, but the house seemed reasonably quiet. Maybe the day's events were just making me edgy. I tiptoed across to the door, and pressed my ear against the wood panelling; but all I could hear was the faint sad moan of the draught that perpetually blew around the house, rattling window sashes and setting chandeliers tinkling, and the usual creaks of floorboards and hinges.

The house was like an old ship at sea, rolling and heaving through a black silent ocean where no fish swam.

A voice whispered: '*Monsieur.*'

I stood slowly away from the door, my mouth salt with shock. I was sure that the voice had come from outside – right outside. It was a dry, sexless voice, the voice of an old woman, or a strange eunuch. I backed off, reaching behind me for the reassurance of my bed, when the voice again said: '*Monsieur.*'

I called hoarsely, 'Who's there? Is that you, father?'

'*Of course,*' answered the voice. '*Who else?*'

'What do you want? It's late.'

'*This is my house. I shall walk where I please.*'

I bit my lip uncertainly. 'Listen,' I said, 'I don't think that you *are* Father Anton.'

'*Who else could I be?*'

'I don't know. Beelzebub?'

The voice cackled. '*Perhaps you ought to open the door and find out.*'

I waited, with my heart taking great irregular gallops under my ribs, and my pulse banging away in sympathy.

73

I heard a shuffling noise outside and then the voice said: '*Monsieur?*'

'What is it?'

'*Open up, monsieur. I have something to show you.*'

'I don't really want to, thanks. Listen, I'm in bed. I'll talk in the morning.'

'*Are you afraid, monsieur?*'

I didn't answer that one. Whatever or whoever it was outside, I didn't want them to know just how frightened I was. I looked around the room for some kind of a weapon, and in the end I picked up a cheap alloy candlestick from the washstand. It wasn't very heavy, but it made me feel better.

The voice said: '*The girl is beautiful, isn't she?*'

'Which girl?'

'*Madeleine.*'

'Can't we talk about it tomorrow? I'm tired. And anyway, I'd like to know who you are.'

The voice laughed. '*I told you. I am Father Anton.*'

'I don't believe you.'

'*You don't believe that priests enjoy sex as much as anyone else? You don't believe that I can look at Madeleine and think of her body? She gets me boiling, monsieur! Oh, yes, she gets me rampant as a goat in the rutting season! Now, don't you feel that way, too?*'

I was shaking with nerves. I took one awkward step towards the door, deliberately stamping my bare foot as loudly as I could on the floorboards, and I shouted: 'Go away! Just get out of here! I don't want to listen!'

There was a pause. A breezy silence. I thought for a moment that the thing might have gone. But then it said, in a treacly, self-satisfied tone, '*I've scared you, haven't I? I've really scared you!*'

'You haven't scared me at all. You're just disturbing my night's rest.'

I felt a vague wind blowing across my room from the direction of the door, and I was certain that I could detect that sour, sickening odour of the demon. Perhaps

74

it was just my imagination. Perhaps I was having a dream. But there I was, defenceless in my nightshirt and my goddamned ridiculous bedsocks, clutching a light-weight candlestick and hoping that whatever whispered behind that door was going to stay behind it, or better still, leave me alone.

'*We must talk, monsieur,*' said the voice.

'I don't think we have anything to talk about.'

'*But of course we do. We must talk about the girl. Don't you want to talk about the girl? Wouldn't you like to sit down for an hour or two, like men of the world, and talk about her bubs, perhaps, or the inner folds of her sex?*'

'Get out of here! I don't want to listen!'

'*But of course you do. You're fascinated. You're fearful, but fascinated. We could talk about the many ways in which girls can have intercourse with animals and reptiles. The pain of it, and the sheer delight! After all, we must have her for the grand gathering, mustn't we? We couldn't do without her.*'

I retreated, trembling, back towards the bed. Whatever stood outside my door, its lewd words seemed to crawl all over me like lice. I groped for, and found, the book of angels which lay on my bedside table; and I also picked up, out of plain old-fashioned superstitious terror, the ring of hair which Eloise had given me for protection against devils and demons.

I raised the book of angels and said tightly: 'I command you to go away. If you don't go away, I'll invoke an angel to drive you away. No matter how dangerous it is, I'll do it.'

The voice chuckled. '*You don't know what you're talking about. Invoke an angel! How can you possibly believe in angels?*'

'The same way I'm beginning to believe in devils.'

'*You think I'm a devil? Well, I'll prove you wrong! Just open the door and I'll show you.*'

I kept the book held high. 'I'm not going to. If you want to talk, talk in the morning. But right now I want you to go. I don't care if you're Father Anton or not. Just go.'

There was a long, dull silence. Then I heard a clicking noise. I couldn't think what it was to begin with, but then I looked again at the door and saw, to my utmost dread, that the key was slowly revolving in the lock. One by one, the lock levers opened; and then the brass bolt at the top of the door slid back as if it was being tugged by a magnet.

My throat constricted. I hefted the candlestick and raised it behind me to hit whatever was out there as hard as I possibly could.

The doorknob turned. The door opened, and that soft sour draught began to course through my bedroom again. Then, untouched, the door swung wide by itself.

Outside, in the corridor, it was totally dark. The house stirred and shifted. I waited and waited, my candlestick raised over my head, but nothing happened. Nobody appeared. Nobody spoke.

I said, 'Are you there?'

There was no reply. I swallowed, and my swallow seemed like the loudest sound in the world.

I took one step forward towards the doorway. Maybe it was waiting for me to come after it. Well, perhaps I shouldn't disappoint it. After all, a demon was only a demon, wasn't it? It was only some croaky voice in the night. Only some whisper in a derelict tank. Nothing more than a scattered heap of bones that Father Anton had sealed in his cellar.

I reached the doorway. The best thing to do would be to jump right out across the corridor. Then, if anything was hiding beside the door, ready to claw out at me, I could turn round and hit it first.

I said, loudly and unsteadily, 'Are you there? Answer me! If you're so damned smart, answer!'

There was nothing. It was so quiet in that moment

that I could hear my watch ticking on the bedside table. I cleared my throat.

I tensed the candlestick in my hand, crouched down a little, and then I threw myself out of the open doorway, across the painted boards of the corridor, and scrambled around so that I was ready with my arm raised and my muscles tightened for action.

There was nothing. The corridor was empty. I felt a shiver that was both fear and relief, intermingled.

Perhaps the best thing to do now would be to go down and check that Father Anton was all right. After all, that whispery voice had claimed to be him, and if it was opening doors all over the house, it could have opened his, too. I pulled up my bedsocks, which were falling down round my ankles, and walked back along the dark corridor as far as the head of the stairs. On the landing below, an old French wallclock was tiredly counting away the small cold hours of the night, and a cardinal with a face about as happy as a hundred-year-old horse was looking gloomily out of an ancient oil painting.

I started to go down the stairs. My nightshirt made a soft sweeping sound on the boards, and I paused once to listen for any unusual noises. The wallclock suddenly whirred and struck the half hour, and I froze. But when the chimes had died away, there was silence again. I walked across the landing, and headed down the corridor where Father Anton's bedroom was.

It was very dark along that corridor. Somehow the atmosphere was different, as if someone else had recently walked down here, disturbing the chilly air. I went as softly as I could, but my own breathing seemed almost deafening, and every floorboard had a creak or a squeak of its own.

I was halfway down the corridor when I saw something down at the far end. I stopped, and strained my eyes. It was difficult to make out what it was in the shadows, but it looked like a child. It was standing with its back to me,

77

apparently gazing out of the small leaded window at the snow-covered yard. I didn't move. The child could have been an illusion – nothing more than an odd composition of light and dark. But from thirty feet away it appeared remarkably real, and I could almost imagine it turning around *and for one moment in my nightmare I had seen a face that grinned like a goat with hideous yellow eyes.*

I took one very cautious step forward. I said: '*You!*' but my voice only came out as a whisper.

The small figure remained still. It was solitary and sad, in a way, like a ghost over whose earthly body no prayers had ever been spoken. It continued to look out over the yard, not moving, not turning, not speaking.

I took one more step nearer, then another. I said: 'Is that you?'

One moment the figure seemed real and tangible, but then as I came even closer, the hooded head became a shadow from the top of the casement, and the small body melted into a triangle of dim light from the snow outside, and I stepped quickly up to the window and saw that there was nobody and nothing there at all.

I looked round, but I knew it was useless. I was so crowded with fears and superstitions that I was seeing things that weren't even there. I walked back to Father Anton's bedroom door, waited for a moment, and then softly knocked.

'Father Anton? It's Dan McCook.'

There was no answer, so I waited for a while and then rapped again.

'Father Anton? Are you awake?'

There was still no answer. I gently tried the door. It wasn't locked, and so I pushed it open and peered into the darkness of his bedroom. It smelled of mothballs and some mentholated rub that he obviously put on his chest at night. On one side was a tall mahogany wardrobe, and on the other was a chest-of-drawers, above which hung a large ebony crucifix with an ivory figure of Christ

78

hanging on it. Father Anton's oak bed was set against the far wall, and I could just make out his pale hand lying on the coverlet, and his white hair on the pillow.

I crept across the worn rug on the floor, and stood a few feet away from him. He had his back turned to me, but he looked all right. I was beginning to think that I was suffering from nightmares and delusions and not enough sleep. I whispered: 'Father Anton?'

He didn't stir, didn't turn around, but a voice said: '*Yes?*'

My grip tightened on my candlestick. It *sounded* like Father Anton, but on the other hand it didn't. It had some of that dry, sardonic quality that I had heard in the voice upstairs. I came a little nearer the bed, and tried to lean over so that I could see Father Anton's face.

'Father Anton? Is that you?'

There was a second's pause. Then Father Anton rose up in his bed as if he was being pulled upright on strings, and he turned to face me with his eyes glassy and his white hair dishevelled. He said, in that same unnatural voice: 'What is it? Why did you wake me?'

I felt there was something curiously and frighteningly wrong. It was the way he was sitting there in his white nightshirt, as if he was unsupported by gravity or anything at all. And it was his peculiar manner, partly calm and partly hostile. There was nothing of the rambling old priest about him. He seemed strangely self-possessed, and his eyes seemed to be observing me as if there was someone else behind them, staring through.

I took a few steps back. 'I think I must have made a mistake,' I said. 'Just a nightmare, that's all.'

'You're frightened,' he said. 'I can tell that you're frightened. Now, why?'

'It's okay,' I told him. 'I guess I just didn't get enough sleep. I'll go right back upstairs now, and I'll—'

'You needn't go. Don't you want to talk? It's very lonesome at this time of night, don't you agree?'

Father Anton's face was rigidly white, and his jaw seemed to move up and down when he spoke with the same mechanical movements of a ventriloquist's dummy. Talking to him right then was like listening to a badly dubbed movie.

'Well, yes,' I said. 'But I'd really rather go. Thanks all the same.'

Father Anton raised a hand. 'You mustn't go.' He turned his head stiffly and looked towards the door. It swung on its hinges, and silently closed, all by itself.

I lifted my candlestick.

'Now then,' admonished Father Anton. 'There's no need to be belligerent. We can be friends, you know. We can help each other.'

I said, quietly: 'You're not Father Anton at all.'

Father Anton abruptly laughed, throwing his head back in a way that terrified me. 'Of course I'm Father Anton. Who do I look like?'

'I don't know. But you're not Father Anton. Now just stay there because I'm getting right out of here and you're not going to stop me.'

Father Anton said: 'Why should I want to stop you? You're a good man and true. You helped me out, so now I'm going to help you.'

I was shivering like a man with pneumonia. I kept the candlestick raised over my head, and I stepped back towards the door. 'Just stay away,' I warned him.

Father Anton gave an awkward, empty shrug. 'You mustn't misunderstand me, *monsieur*.'

'I understand you all right. I don't know what you are, or what you're trying to do, but keep away.'

The old priest's eyes glittered. 'If we don't find the other twelve, you know, we could be in terrible trouble.'

'The other twelve what?'

'The other twelve *brethren*. There are thirteen of us, you know. I told you that. Thirteen of us. We have been separated for such a long time, and now we must get together again.'

I kept on shuffling my way backwards. 'You don't know where they are?' I asked him.

Father Anton swayed. Then he looked up oddly and said, 'They've been hidden. They've been sewn up and sealed, just like before. I was the only one who wasn't taken with them. Now you must help me find them. You and the girl together. We need the girl.'

I shook my head tautly. 'I'm not going to help you find or do anything. I'm getting right out of here and I'm going to get some help.'

Father Anton lifted one jerky leg out from under the bedclothes, then the other. He stood up unsteadily, his arms hanging by his sides, and he grinned at me. For a split second, I thought I saw a thin dark tongue flick from his mouth – a tongue as forked as a reptile's – but then it flicked back again and I wasn't sure if it was just an illusion or not.

'We will have to find the Reverend Taylor in England,' said Father Anton, in a soft, rustling voice. 'Then we will have to discover where the Americans hid the rest of us. My lord Adramelech will be deeply pleased, I can assure you. He will reward you, *monsieur*, in a way that no man on earth has ever been rewarded before. You can be rich beyond any comprehension. You can be powerful as a thousand men. You can spend years indulging your tastes for the finest foods and the greatest wines. And you can have sex with any woman, any man, any animal, you choose, and your virility will be limitless.'

I didn't know what to say or do. It seemed as though Father Anton had been completely taken over. But was he really possessed, or was he just suffering from nightmarish nerves? Maybe he'd taken too many heart pills, or drunk too much before he went to bed. I just couldn't look at this elderly shambling priest in his long white nightshirt and believe that I was talking to a devil.

Father Anton took one staggering step towards me. I retreated even further.

'Father Anton,' I said, 'you're sick. Now, why don't you lie down for a moment, and I'll go and get a doctor.'

'Sick?' he hissed, 'I'm not sick. I'm free.'

'Will you stay back, please?' I asked him. 'I'n going to have to hit you if you come any nearer, and I don't want to do that.'

'You amuse me,' whispered the priest. 'But I am never amused for long. Father Anton was not amusing. Fortunately, he was weak. A man who believes in us is so much more susceptible than a man who doesn't.'

'You took over Father Anton? You possessed him?'

'You could say so, yes.'

'What does that mean?'

Father Anton took another step nearer. 'Possession is more physical than mental. I possess Father Anton now, because I am inside Father Anton.'

I went cold with foreboding. I said: 'I don't understand you. What do you mean – you're *inside* Father Anton?'

The white-dressed priest came clumsily towards me. His expression was grey and blank, and apart from those dark, penetrating eyes, I might have been looking at a corpse.

'A man, like a demon, is a mechanical device,' he said, in a voice that was even less like Father Anton's than before, and so much like the voice that I had heard in the tank that I *knew* – despite everything I was trying to do to persuade myself otherwise – that this was the devil we had tried to seal in the cellar, the disciple of Adramelech who had once brought plague and misery to Rouen.

I said nothing. I guessed I was five or six paces away from the door now. The old priest kept stepping woodenly towards me.

'From inside, I can manipulate his legs and his arms like a marionette,' said the devil. 'I can look through the sockets of his eyes, and breathe through the cavities of his nostrils. It's a secure home inside here, *monsieur*. Warm and bloody, and sweet with decay already. I could even seduce that shrivelled old housekeeper of his through his own dangling penis!'

I stared at the priest with mounting fright.

'Are you lying?' I taxed him, knowing he wasn't. 'My God, if you're lying—'

'Your God won't help you. He didn't help Father Anton.'

'Well, where *is* Father Anton?' I demanded. 'What have you done with him?'

The stiff figure marched so close that I could have reached out and touched him.

He said, in that coarse, throaty voice, 'You're almost standing in him.'

At first. I didn't want to take my eyes off the devil. But then I glanced quickly down behind me, and I saw something that made my stomach tighten and turn over. On the floor beside the chest-of-drawers, spread out in pale mucus-coloured strings, clotted with dark-red kidneys and blueish cakes of liver, were Father Anton's entrails. The devil had disembowelled him, and climbed into his empty body like some hideous kind of parasite.

The devil hadn't moved. I looked back at it in fear and nausea, and said: 'You've killed him.'

The devil grunted in evil amusement. 'On the contrary, I think I've given the old fool some new life. He was almost dead anyway. His heart wouldn't have lasted much longer, particularly after you dragged him out in all that snow.'

I paused, anxiously biting my lip. If the devil could rip Father Anton open, it could certainly do something equally disgusting to me. I looked quickly up at the ebony crucifix on the wall, and wondered if everything I'd seen in vampire movies was true. Was it really possible to ward off demons and ghosts with the Holy Cross?

Sidestepping Father Anton's glutinous remains, I reached over the chest-of-drawers and wrenched down the crucifix. Then I brandished it right in the devil's face, and shouted as heroically as I could: '*I dismiss you! In the name of the Lord, I dismiss you!*'

With one powerful blow, the old priest knocked the crucifix out of my hand. He gave a hissing snarl, and moved towards me again, his eyes as dark and cruel as an alligator's.

I swung my arm back, and belted him across the side of the face with my candlestick. His head jerked to one side, and the base of the candlestick raised a weal; but no blood flowed because Father Anton's heart wasn't pumping any longer, and his occupied cadaver simply shuddered and stepped forward again.

'Your violence amuses me,' it whispered. 'Now let's see if *mine* amuses *you*.'

I edged back. I knew that I'd never make the door in time. I kept my eyes on Father Anton's grey, bruised face, and I began to wish that I'd never seen that damned tank, and never dreamed of opening it.

'It's such a pity, you know,' said Father Anton. 'You could have assisted me so much. But I have only survived the centuries by protecting myself against the moral and the conscientious, and I'm afraid that I shall have to deal with you as I have dealt with so many others.'

I only had one gambit left. I reached into the pocket of my nightshirt and produced the small ring of hair which Eloise had given me, the hair which was supposed to prove that I had already paid my dues to the hierarchy of hell.

There was an electric silence. Father Anton raised his eyes and stared at the hair with undisguised malevolence. I thought for a moment that he was going to tear the hair aside, just like the crucifix. But then that forked tongue flickered again, and the demon moved warily aside, watching me with a hard, poisonous look that made me so nervous I could hardly speak.

'Well,' said Father Anton, keeping his eyes on the ring of hair. 'I see that you're less *naif* than I thought. You're not a witch, or a necromancer, and yet you keep the first-born's locks with you. Now, I wonder how you got hold of them?'

'That's none of your business. Just keep back.'

Father Anton jerkily raised his hands in a gesture of conciliation. 'There is no need for us to quarrel, *monsieur*. There is no need for us to fight. After all, you must remember that you can protect yourself only *once* with this ring of hair; and for each protection thereafter you will need to sacrifice some other first-born to Moloch. It will only take the rising of tomorrow's sun, and its setting at evening, and all the power you have in that ring will have died with the day.'

'I'm not interested. I'll have you behind bars by then.'

Father Anton threw back his head again, and laughed. Then, without warning, the door banged wide open and slammed shut again, and the windows exploded in a hailstorm of shattered glass. The sheets were whipped off the bed in a screaming indoor hurricane, and the furniture was thrown violently around the room, clattering and bumping.

Most hideous of all, Father Anton's body was hurled this way and that, its arms flailing wildly in all directions, until there was a shrieking blast of wind, and it was thrown face-first into his dressing-table mirror, the sharp slices of glass opening up his face like a skinned chicken.

The noise died away. I lowered my arm away from my eyes. The room was very dark now, although the curtains were flapping open, and a grey strained light was reflected from the snow outside. With the windows broken, it was intensely cold.

Something small and shadowy was sitting in the far corner of the room, on the oaken post of Father Anton's bed. I couldn't make it out very well, but I could see stubs of horns and eyes that slanted like a goat's. It made a dry, leathery sound as it shifted on its perch.

'*Monsieur*,' it whispered.

'What is it?' I asked, chilled.

'I must warn you, *monsieur*, not to interfere again. Next time, you will have no protection.'

'There isn't going to *be* any next time,' I asserted.

'*Monsieur*,' said the devil, 'I am going to find my brethren with or without your assistance. Although, if you have any taste for what is best for you, you will do what you can to help me.'

'What about Madeleine?'

'She must come too.'

'That's out of the question.'

The devil rustled, papery and ancient as Hell itself.

'I will strike a bargain with you,' it whispered. 'If you help me to find my brethren, you and Madeleine, then I will restore this fool to life.'

'That's insane.'

The devil laughed. 'Insanity is a human word which almost always describes the activities of devils. Yes, in that sense, it is insane. But Adramelech can do it.'

'How about you? Can you do it?'

'It is not within my powers.'

I hefted my candlestick again. I wondered what the devil was capable of doing in the time it would take me to cross the room and smash him off his perch.

I said: 'I thought only God could give the gift of life.'

The devil shifted its unseen claws. 'Life is not a gift, my friend. It is a curse. Adramelech is quite capable of giving such a curse.'

My mouth felt very dry. I said: 'How can I believe you? How can I trust you?'

There was a moment's pause. The winter wind raised and lowered the drapes, and flakes of snow came tumbling over the window-ledge. The devil stirred, and said in that

86

throaty, sexless voice: 'You don't doubt what I can do, surely?'

I moved cautiously across the rumpled rug, trying to get as near to the devil as I could.

'I doubt your existence,' I said. 'I doubt if you're anything more than a nightmare.'

The devil cackled. 'Then watch,' it said. 'Just watch.'

There was a silence. The shadows of the drapes rose and fell, like the wings of dreadful creatures. Then the house was pierced by a high, hideous shriek, and I heard furniture falling, glass breaking; and someone keening and moaning like an animal in agony. I turned. The door banged open again. From out of the corridor came a low, howling wind, and then the sound of someone staggering towards us, mumbling in pain as it came.

There was a crackle of electricity, and the whole room was dazzlingly lit by a blueish light. Then there was darkness again, and a rumble of thunder that compressed my eardrums and almost threw me over. Then there was another fierce blitz of electricity, even brighter than the first, and in the wide-open doorway, her arms raised in desperation, her face blotted white by the demonic lightning, I saw Antoinette, the elderly maid, in a nightdress soaked by torrents of blood, her whole body, her arms, her legs, her stomach, her face, porcupined with knives and forks and scissors and skewers. It was as if every sharp instrument in the whole house had flown from its drawer and stabbed itself into her.

Her voice almost swallowed by another burst of thunder, she moaned: '*Father Anton, save me . . .*' and collapsed to her knees with a clatter of knife and scissor handles.

I turned back to the devil, and I was stunned and furious. 'Is *that* your damned power? Slaughtering old women? You damned maniac!'

The voice came from somewhere else now – on top of

the dark mahogany wardrobe, in a corner where I couldn't see.

'You would consider it powerful if it happened to you, *monsieur*. Or if it happened to Madeleine. I could make it happen to Madeleine right now. Every pitchfork and castrating knife in the whole of her farm could stick itself into her right now, right this minute. You only have to say the word.'

I said, quaking: 'What are you? What kind of a devil are you?'

The devil laughed. 'I am Elmek, sometimes known as Asmorod, the devil of knives and sharp edges. I am the devil of swords and daggers and razors. Do you like my work, you with your blunt cudgel and your blunt anger?'

I hurled my candlestick towards the shadows where the devil's voice came from, but it clattered uselessly against the wardrobe door, and dropped to the floor.

'You have a choice, *monsieur*,' the devil said. 'You can either help me or try to hinder me. If you help me, Adramelech will reward you. If you hinder me, these dead will remain dead, and I will make sure that your precious Madeleine is sliced up like so much meat.'

I pressed my hands to my forehead. I could hear Antoinette gurgling and choking in her own blood, but there was nothing I could do. If I tried to fight this devil any longer, it was going to cut everyone to pieces, including Madeleine and Eloise and Jacques Passerelle, and once the sun had risen and set, it would probably cut me to pieces, too. I knew then that I was going to have to pacify this demon, and play for as much time as I could get. If we searched for its brethren, it's twelve brother devils, it could take us months, and by that time I might have found some way to exorcise it for good.

I lowered my eyes, trying to look resigned and obedient. I said: 'All right. It's a bargain. What do you want me to do?'

The devil rustled in pleasure. 'I thought you might see sense. You *are* a good man and true, aren't you?'

'I'm just trying to save people's lives,' I told him.

'Of course. Very commendable. Life is full of commendable deeds, and it's such a pity that they usually cause so much pain. I am the devil of suicide by throat-cutting or slashing of wrists, did you know that? I am always honoured when someone slices himself up nicely.'

'Just tell me what to do.'

'Of course,' said the devil. 'All in good time.'

'What am I going to do with these bodies? What if the police ask me about them?'

'That's very simple. When we have left, the house will burn. Not a severe blaze, but enough to gut this room, and the room along the corridor where this lady slept. It will be a great tragedy. Everybody will be sorry that their old priest is dead, but he was senile, wasn't he, and perhaps he let the candle fall on his bedspread, or a stray log drop on to his rug. Nobody will think to question you. You will have had no motive for arson, and so nobody will suspect your involvement.'

'For Christ's sake, I didn't kill them anyway!'

The devil laughed. 'How many murderers have said that! How many witches have protested their innocence! How many Nazis claimed they were only obeying their orders!'

I shut my mouth tight, and told myself, silently and firmly, to keep my fear and my anger bottled up tight. If this devil ever suspected that I was trying to play it along, it would probably cut me up like shish-kebabs in a split-second. I still couldn't get that sickening apparition of Antoinette out of my mind, and I knew that I was going to have nightmares about those forests of knives and scissors for the rest of my life. There was no sound, now, from the doorway. I guessed she was probably dead.

'How are we going to get you to England?' I asked the devil

Elmek was silent for a moment. Then it said: 'There is a copper-and-lead-bound trunk in the cellar. It was first used for carrying sacramental robes and chalices in the days when the king travelled around the countryside, staying at the chateaux of French barons. I will enjoy the irony of travelling in it myself. You will arrange for transportation across the Channel this afternoon, and all you will have to do is collect the trunk from the cellar and take it with you.'

'Supposing I deliberately forget? Supposing I leave you behind?'

'Then these two people will remain as dead as they are now, and your precious Madeleine will have the nastiest death I can devise. And so will you.'

Outside the shattered window, the sky was growing greyer as dawn approached. I said: 'All right. If that's what you want.'

'That's precisely what I want. I am looking forward to meeting the Reverend Taylor again.'

I stood in the ruined room, wondering what I ought to do next. I kept the ring of hair curled around my finger, and I couldn't even bear to look at the carnage around me. I felt a sourish, bilious taste in my mouth.

The devil said: 'You can go now. Get dressed. The sooner you arrange our journey, the better.'

I looked up at the gloomy corner where it was hidden. I said: 'If I disbelieved in you – if I refuted your very existence – would you disappear?'

Elmek laughed once again. 'If I disbelieved in *you*,' it said, 'if I refuted *your* very existence, would *you* disappear?'

I wiped my soiled and sweaty face with my hand, and I felt about as desperate and depressed as I ever had in my whole life.

I reached the Passerelle's farm just after seven, in a chill, thick fog. I parked the Citroën in the muddy yard, walked across to the stable door, and knocked. A black-and-white dog with matted fur came and sniffed at my knees, and then loped off round the side of the farm buildings.

Jacques Passerelle appeared at the door, wiping his hands on a towel. His braces were hanging from his belt, and he still had a blob of white shaving cream clinging to his left ear. He was smoking one of his Gauloises and coughing.

'Mr McCook, *qu'est-ce que c'est qui se passe?*'

'Is Madeleine here? It's rather urgent.'

'She's milking. Round the side there, third door. You look bad. A night on the tiles?'

I grimaced. 'Would you believe I spent a night with Father Anton?'

Jacques laughed. 'These priests! They're worse than the rest of us!'

I stepped around the thickest ruts of mud until I reached the cowshed door. It was warm and musky in there, scented with the breath of cows. Madeleine was perched on a stool, wearing a blue scarf around her head, jeans, and muddy rubber boots. Her hands worked expertly at the cow's teats, and the thin jets of milk rang against the sides of the zinc pail. I leaned against the door for a while, and then I said: 'Madeleine.'

She looked up, surprised. In her work clothes, she had a casual, *gamine* attractiveness that, in normal circumstances, I couldn't have resisted. She said: 'Dan! *Quelle heure est-il?*'

'Ten past seven.'

'Why have you come so early? Is anything wrong?'

I nodded, trying to keep my shock and nausea under control. I said: 'I don't know how to tell you.'

She let go of the cow's udder, and set the pail down on the cobbled floor. Her face was pale and strained, and it looked as if she hadn't slept a lot more than I had

She said: 'Is it Father Anton? Is he all right?'

I shook my head.

'He's not—?'

I was so exhausted that I leaned my head against the frame of the cowshed door, and when I spoke I could only manage a dull, tired monotone. I felt as if I'd been gutted, like a herring, and left to drain on somebody's sink.

'The devil broke out somehow. I heard it in the night. I went downstairs and it had killed Father Anton. Then it killed Antoinette in front of my eyes, to prove its power.'

Madeleine came across the shed and touched my shoulder. 'Dan – you're not serious. Please.'

I lifted my head and looked at her. 'How serious do I have to be? I was there. I saw the devil cut Father Anton open, and I saw him kill Antoinette. It says its name is Elmek, the devil of sharp knives. It said that if we didn't help it find its brethren, it would cut us to pieces as well.'

'I can't believe what you're saying.'

'Well, you'd better damn well believe it, because it's true! If you don't want to wind up like Antoinette, you'd better find some way of making your excuses to your father and getting yourself an indefinite vacation.'

She frowned. 'What do you mean?'

'I mean that all the time we have is the time that devil decides to grant us. It insists we help it find its brethren, and we're only going to stay alive as long as we appear to be co-operating. It wants to leave for England this afternoon. If we leave at eight, we can just catch the ferry at Dieppe.'

Madeleine looked completely confused. 'Dan, I can't just walk out of here! What can I say to papa? I'm supposed to be here to help!'

I was so tired and upset that I was near to tears. 'Madeleine,' I insisted, 'I wouldn't ask you if it wasn't deadly serious. If *you* won't make your excuses to your father, then *I'll* have to go and tell him the truth.'

'But Dan, it seems so *unreal*.'

'Don't you think I feel the same way?' I asked her.

'Don't you think I'd rather get on with my damned work and forget this thing ever happened? But I've seen it for myself, Madeleine. It's real, and we're both in danger of death.'

Those pale Norman eyes regarded me seriously. Then Madeleine slowly pulled the scarf from her hair, and said: 'You mean it.'

'Yes, I damned well mean it.'

She looked out of the cowshed across the foggy yard. Over the hills, behind the dim tracery of leafless elms, the sun glowered through the grey haze of another winter day in the Suisse Normande.

'Very well,' she said. 'I'll go and tell my father. I can pack in half an hour.'

I followed her through a flock of grubby geese and into the farmhouse. Jacques Passerelle was in the red-tiled hallway, combing his short hair into a neat parting. Madeleine came up behind him and held him round the waist. He glanced up at her face in the mirror and smiled.

'You've finished the milking already?' he asked her.

She shook her head. 'I'm afraid that Dan came with an urgent message. I have to spend a little time in England.'

He frowned. '*Angleterre? Pourquoi?*'

Madeleine lowered her eyes. 'I can't lie. It's something to do with the tank. We have to go and find some information for Father Anton.'

Jacques turned around and held his daughter's arms. 'The tank? Why do you have to go to England because of the tank?'

'Because of the English priest, father. The Reverend Taylor, who was here in the war. He is the only man who really knows about the tank, and what was inside it.'

I put in: 'We won't be away long, *Monsieur* Passerelle. Maybe a week at the outside. Then I promise I'll bring her straight back.'

Jacques rubbed his shiny shaven chin. 'I don't know

what to say. All this tank seems to bring is trouble and more trouble.'

I said, 'Believe me, *monsieur*, this is going to be the last of it. Once we're back from England, you won't ever hear about that tank again. Not ever.'

Jacques Passerelle sniffed. He didn't seem to be particularly impressed by that. He turned to Madeleine and asked: 'Why does it have to be you? Can't Mr McCook go by himself? It always seems that you have to do the work that others should do. And what about Father Anton?'

Madeleine looked across at me appealingly. I knew she didn't want to leave her father to cope by himself in the middle of winter. But I shook my head. The last thing I was going to do was cross that devil again. My ring of hair was going to protect me only until the sun set, and then I would be as vulnerable as Madeleine.

'*Monsieur*,' I told him, 'we really have to go, both of us. I'm sorry.'

The farmer sighed. 'Very well, if that's what you have to do. I will call Gaston Jumet and ask him if Henriette can come up and help me. You said a week, no more?'

'About a week,' I told him, although I had no idea how long it was going to take us to dig up Elmek's twelve infamous brethren.

'Very well,' he said, and kissed his daughter, and shook my hand. 'If this is something really important. Now, would you like some calvados and coffee?'

While Madeleine packed, I sat at the kitchen table with Jacques and Eloise. Outside, it began to snow again – thin, wet snow that dribbled slowly down the window panes. We talked about farming and cows and what to do when turnips started to mildew in the ground.

After a while, Jacques Passerelle knocked back his calvados, wiped his mouth with his spotted handkerchief, and said: 'I must get to work. We have two fields to plough by the end of the week. I wish you *bon voyage*.'

We shook hands and then he went off into the hallway to pull on his wellingtons and his thick jacket. I stirred my coffee carefully, waiting until he was out of earshot, and then I said, 'Eloise?'

The old woman nodded. 'I know.'

'You know? How do you know?'

She said nothing, but reached in the pocket of her apron, and produced a worn sepia photograph of a young cleric. He was holding a boater in his hands, and squinting into the sun.

I looked at the picture for a long while, and then I said: 'This is Father Anton.'

'Yes, *monsieur*. I have known him for many years. When we were young, we were close friends. We were so close, in fact, that we hardly had to speak to know what each other was thinking. Well, Father Anton reached me last night, after a fashion. I woke in the night and felt that I had lost him; and when I saw you this morning, I knew that he was dead.'

'You didn't tell Jacques?'

'I told nobody. I wasn't really sure it was true. I hoped that it wasn't. But then I saw you, and I knew.'

I took out the ring of hair which she had given me. 'Listen, Eloise,' I asked her, 'is this all the hair you have?'

She lifted her grey head and looked at me closely through her flour-dusted spectacles. 'You want more? Why?'

'The devil is loose, Eloise. It was the devil who killed Father Anton. That's why we're going to England. The devil insists.'

'Insists?'

'If we don't do what it says, it's going to stab us to death. Madeleine and me. Its name is Elmek, the devil of knives.'

Eloise took the photograph of Father Anton from me with shaking hands. She was so agitated that she couldn't speak at first, and I poured her a small glass of calvados.

She drank half of it, and coughed, and then looked back at me with a face so ghastly with strain that I felt frightened myself.

'Did he suffer?' she whispered. 'Did poor Father Anton suffer?'

'I don't know. I don't think so. But I saw Antoinette die too, his housekeeper, and she was in terrible pain.'

'What's going to happen? What are we going to do?'

'There's not much we can do except what we're told. The devil is going to burn the bodies so that nobody knows what happened – and Eloise, it's desperately important that you don't tell them.'

Eloise was weeping. 'What about Madeleine?' she said, wiping her eyes with her apron. 'It won't hurt Madeleine, will it?'

I took her hand. 'It won't if we do what it tells us to do. I have to find out how to destroy it first, how to exorcise it. Meanwhile, we're going to have to go along with it, and help it find its twelve brethren.'

Eloise said: 'There is only one thing I can do to help you. Wait for one moment.'

She rose stiffly from her chair and walked across the tiled floor to the kitchen dresser. She opened a drawer, fumbled around for a while with tins and jars and boxes, and eventually took out a small tin with the name of a popular brand of French throat pastilles printed on it. She brought it over to the table and carefully lifted the lid.

I peered inside. There was nothing there but a small heap of what looked like grey powder.

'What's this?' I asked her.

She closed the lid again, and handed the tin to me. 'It is said to be the ashes of the seamless cloak which Christ wore when he was crucified. It is the most powerful relic I have.'

'What will it do? Will it protect us?'

'I don't know. Some relics have real magical properties

96

and some are simply frauds. It is all I can do. It is all I can give you.'

She turned away then, her eyes filled with tears. I didn't know what to do to comfort her. I slipped the tin of ashes in my pocket and finished my coffee. The clock on the kitchen wall struck eight; I knew that if we were going to make the lunchtime ferry to Newhaven, we were going to have to hurry.

Madeleine came downstairs with her suitcase. I got up from the table and took it from her, and gave Eloise a last affectionate pat on the shoulder.

Madeleine said: 'What's the matter? Why is Eloise crying?'

'She knows about Father Anton. And she's worried that the same thing's going to happen to you.'

Madeleine leaned over the old woman and kissed her. 'Don't worry,' she said. 'We won't be gone long. Mr McCook will look after me.'

Eloise nodded miserably.

'Come on,' I said, 'we're going to be late.'

We went out into the yard, and I stowed Madeleine's suitcase in the back of the 2CV. The thin snow fell on us like a wet veil. We only had one more piece of luggage to collect – the medieval trunk from the cellar of Father Anton's house. We climbed into the car and I started the engine. Then we bounced off along the narrow, icy roads, the car's heater blaring, and the windshield wipers squeaking backwards and forwards.

Although the French rise early, the village was still deserted by the time we reached Father Anton's house and pulled up in the front yard. I got out of the car, walked round, and opened Madeleine's door for her.

'What do we need here?' she asked me, stepping out.

'The devil,' I said gravely. 'We're taking it with us.'

'Taking it with us? I don't understand.'

'Just come and help me. I'll tell you what it's all about later.'

Madeleine looked up at the house. She could see the broken window of Father Anton's bedroom, with the curtains flapping and twisting in the cold wind. She said: 'Is Father Anton up there? And Antoinette?'

I nodded. 'We have to be quick. As soon as we leave, the devil's going to set the house alight.'

Madeleine crossed herself. 'We should call the police, Dan. We can't just let this happen.'

I took her wrist, and pulled her towards the house.

'Dan, we ought to! I can't bear to leave Father Anton this way!'

'Listen,' I told her bluntly, 'we don't have any choice. If we don't do what Elmek tells us, we're going to die like them. Can you understand that? And besides, it's Father Anton's only chance of survival, too.'

I unlocked the heavy front door and pushed it open.

'What do you mean?' she said. 'He's dead. How can he have a chance of survival?'

I looked at her straight. 'Because I made a bargain. If we help Elmek to find his twelve brethren, and the thirteen brethren between them raise the demon Adramelech, then it will ask Adramelech to bring Father Anton and Antoinette back to life.'

Madeleine stared at me. 'You don't believe that – surely?'

'What else can I believe? I saw the devil, Madeleine. I saw it with my own eyes. I saw Antoinette covered in knives. I saw Father Anton cut open like a beef carcass.'

'Oh, God,' she said, in a low, haunted voice. 'I can't go through with it.'

'You have to. Now, come on.'

Together, we walked down the echoing length of the polished hallway. I took the cellar key down from its hook, unlocked the cellar door, and led Madeleine down into the musty darkness. At the foot of the stairs I found a lightswitch, and turned it on.

The copper-and-lead trunk was waiting for us. It was

98

an ancient, dull-coloured rectangular chest, locked with three copper hasps. It must have been six or seven hundred years old, and it was decorated with copper inlays of horses and helmeted riders, and fleurs-de-lys.

Madeleine whispered: 'Is that it? Is the devil in there?'

I nodded. 'You're going to have to help me lift it. Do you think you can manage?'

'I've been milking cows and mucking-out stables for weeks. I think I'm strong enough.'

Full of foreboding, we approached the trunk and stood beside it. Then we took its curved handles in both hands, and slowly lifted it off the cellar floor. It was staggeringly heavy. It must have weighed all of two hundred and twenty pounds, dead weight, and we had to drag it and slide it across to the stairs. Then we hefted it up, step by step, until we reached the hallway.

It was a matter of three or four minutes to get the trunk out of the house and into the yard. I opened up the Citroën's rear door, ready to receive it but I was just rearranging my own cases, when Madeleine said: 'Look! Just look at that!'

Where the trunk rested, the snow was melting. No snow settled on top of it, either. It was almost as if the snow was shrinking away from our evil and malevolent burden in fear.

'One last heave,' I said dryly, and we lifted the trunk into the back of the Citroën. Then I checked my watch. If we took the Route Nationale from Caen, we could be in Dieppe in about three hours. I shut and locked the back of the car, and we climbed in and settled ourselves down.

I said to Madeleine, softly: 'You don't have to go through with this if you don't want to. I mean, if you don't really believe this devil's going to hurt you, you could take a risk and stay at home.'

'What do you mean?'

I shrugged. 'I'm not sure. But I've always felt that any

kind of devil only has as much power as you're prepared to concede it. If we weren't afraid of Elmek, then maybe it couldn't hurt us.'

Madeleine shook her head. I believe in this devil, Dan. I've believed in it longer than you have. And I started all this terrible killing, too, so I think I have a duty to see it through.'

'It's your choice,' I told her, and switched on the engine. Then I pulled out of the snowbound yard, and drove through the cold, empty streets of Pont D'Ouilly. I kept glancing in my mirror at the dull shape of the medieval trunk – and also to see if any smoke was rising yet out of Father Anton's house. But the trunk remained silent and closed, and it only took a few minutes of driving down those winding roads before the village disappeared behind the trees and the hills, and I never saw Elmek's strange powers at work.

Madeleine said: 'I'm sorry, Dan. If I'd only known.'

'We'll beat them yet,' I told her. 'Elmek and Adramelech and the whole damned team.'

But when I looked again at the sinister bulk of that ancient trunk, I felt far from confident; and I couldn't even guess at what hideous atrocities its nightmarish inhabitant was already scheming.

A French onion-seller wavered across the road in front of me on his bicycle, and I blew my horn at him angrily.

'*Cochon!*' he shouted, and shook his fist as he dwindled out of sight in the snow.

Dieppe was as grey and tatty as any Channel port, and we only stopped in the cobbled square in the centre of town for a few minutes, just to change some French francs into British pounds. It was almost lunchtime, and we were lucky to make the bank before it closed. In France, they take their lunch seriously. Then we drove out to the SNCF ferry, past the cluttered little cafés and tourist arcades and bars called 'Le Bar Anglais' or 'Le

Bar Churchill', where day-tripping British tourists spent their last few francs on very ordinary *vin ordinaire*; past the cranes and the docks and the clutter of crates and trucks; until we turned the corner and saw the black-and-white ship with its red-painted funnel, and the English Channel the colour of pale green soup.

I bought tickets, and we waited nervously in line for twenty minutes before our Citroën was waved down the metal ramp into the bowels of the ship. We parked the car in a jampack of Mercedes and Audis and Renaults, and then climbed to the upper decks to wait out the three-and-a-half hour journey.

The trip across the Channel to Newhaven is one of the dullest sea voyages there is. We went into the ferry's restaurant, and ate leek soup and veal with congealed gravy, while the ship's engines drummed and the sea rose and tipped outside the salt-stained windows.

Madeleine said: 'You're very quiet.'

I mopped up soup with a piece of stale French bread. 'I was thinking about last night.'

'Was it really terrible?'

'I was scared stiff, if that's what you mean.'

She looked out of the window. 'Do you think we can exorcise it? Do you think there's any way?'

'Well, maybe the Reverend Woodfall Taylor will know the answer to that – if the Reverend Woodfall Taylor's still alive.'

'Oh, God, I hope so.'

They brought the meat and a selection of overcooked vegetables. At least they had a decent wine – a bottle of rich, heady Margaux that almost sent me to sleep with its fumes. I ate because I was hungry, but every mouthful was like balsa wood.

Madeleine said: 'Couldn't we simply throw the trunk over the side?'

I sipped my wine. 'I suppose we could do. But I don't think devils drown, do you? And what if he killed us before we could throw him over? Or after? And apart from any of those problems, the ship's crew would probably stop us. I shouldn't think they're very keen on people tossing strange boxes into the Channel.'

She put down her fork, although she had hardly touched her veal.

'Dan,' she said, 'I'm frightened.'

'You have every right to be.'

'No, Dan, I mean *really* frightened. Like something awful is going to happen.'

I looked at her over the rim of my wine glass, and there was nothing I could say. I couldn't pretend that things were going to get better, because it looked as if they were going to get worse. I couldn't even pretend I had a plan to get us out of trouble. All I was doing was playing for time, with the terrible knowledge that Elmek was probably going to sacrifice both of us to Adramelech in any case. Why should he keep his bargain, if he could cut us to shreds by magic at any time he chose, and we were powerless? The ship rolled steadily, and the cutlery and cruets and glasses and ashtrays all rattled and jingled and vibrated in a ceaseless cantata.

Later, we stood by the rail and watched the whitish smudge of England appear on the port side – the seven chalk cliffs they call the Seven Sisters, sloping gradually down on the westward side towards Seaford beach and Newhaven harbour. The ferry turned herself round to back stern-first into the narrow harbour entrance, and a barely intelligible French voice told us over the intercom to return to our cars.

We were both depressed and fearful as we went down the stairs to the car decks and unwillingly rejoined our hellish charge. Neither of us spoke as we sat waiting for the stern doors of the ship to open up, and neither of us looked around at that dark medieval trunk in which the devil nestled. I felt unbearably claustrophobic inside that ship, as if tons of metal were pressing down on me from up above.

At last, the crew waved us out of the ferry and up the ramp to the dockside. It was one of those bright, grey afternoons, with a damp sea-breeze blowing. A cheerful-looking customs official beckoned us towards a vacant inspection bay, and we drove in and stopped.

Madeleine opened her window, and the customs official leaned in. He had that relentless urbanity that always disturbs me in British excise officers – a little different from the laconic gum-chewing lady in the fur coat who always insists you open up all your bags at JFK. He said: 'How long do you plan to stay in Britain, sir?'

'I don't know. About a week. Maybe two.'

'Holiday?'

'Yes, that's right.'

He shaded his eyes against the reflection from our window glass, and peered into the back of the car. Then he walked all the way around, and came up to my window. I opened it, and sat there with what I hoped was a calm, obliging smile. I probably looked like Sylvester the cat when Tweety-Pie's bulldog pal suddenly appears in the garden – all clenched teeth and sick grin.

The customs official said: 'Do you know that it is a serious offence to try to smuggle live animals into the United Kingdom, sir?'

I nodded like an idiot. 'Yes, I knew that. Something to do with rabies, right?'

'That's right, sir. Now, would you care to tell me what you have in that box?'

'Box? Oh, you mean that trunk.'

'Yes, sir.'

'Well, that's just a few odd bits and pieces. I collect antiques. I have a few books in there, a couple of statuettes. Bits and pieces.'

The customs official made a note on his clipboard. Then he pointed with his ballpen to a side bay where a

103

couple of Germans were already having their Mercedes thoroughly searched. He was just about to say something when he frowned, and looked back at me, and then looked around as if he'd lost something.

I said, 'Is everything all right?'

He shook his head, as if it was foggy. 'Yes, sir. I just had the feeling I was going to say something. I can't remember what it was.'

I licked my lips tensely, and glanced over at Madeleine. Neither of us said a word.

The customs official said: 'Very good, sir. Have a pleasant time,' and stuck a label on the Citroën's windshield. I started the engine up, and we drove out of the docks and into the town. It was only when we were out of sight of the cranes and the ships that I let out a long whistle of relief.

Madeleine whispered: 'The devil must have *known* what was going to happen! Did you see what it did to that man's mind? It wiped him *clean*.'

I took a quick look round at the dull lead-coloured trunk. I was beginning to feel so nervous about it now that I kept imagining itches on my skin, and my right eye flickered with a tic that I couldn't control. I didn't dare try to imagine what that thing inside it really looked like. I had seen enough in the darkness of Father Anton's bedroom, and heard enough of its rustling body and scratching claws and its husky, evil voice.

We drove aimlessly around the town of Newhaven, which wasn't much more salubrious than Dieppe. Mean, red-roofed houses with primrose-painted gates. Ware-houses and shops. Madeleine said, 'What are we going to do now?'

'I don't know. Find a place to stay, I guess.'

She checked her watch. 'I think we ought to try to find where the Reverend Taylor lives before we do that. The pubs are open now. Let's have a drink and something to eat, and then we can go to the local library. They have a clerical directory called Crockford's in England, and if he's still alive, we'll find his name in there.'

We parked the Citroën in a municipal car park, and crossed the road to a big, dingy Victorian pub called The Prince of Wales, which smelled of spilled beer and cooking fat. We sat by the engraved-glass window drinking some tepid Skol lager, and eating cold sausage rolls with no sausage in them. Gastronomically speaking, England is always a miserable experience after France. Mine host behind the bar was a fat fellow with a check shirt and walrus moustache, who kept pulling pints of beer for himself and discussing the relative merits of the A23 and the A24, which turned out to be roads. One of the Englishman's greatest obsessions, after cricket scores, is route-planning; and when you see the roads you know why.

After our drink, we went in search of the library. It turned out to be a small brick building not far from the car park, where a spinster in a pale-blue cardigan and upswept glasses was almost ready to close for the night. She found a copy of Crockford's Clerical Directory for us, and brought it over to the checking-out table with a face as long-suffering as a Rhesus monkey with a mouthful of vinegar. We flicked through the pages as quickly as we could, while she pulled on her coat, and huffed, and tugged on her gloves, and huffed again, and switched off all the lights at the far end of the room.

But after a quick search through the directory, we found what we were looking for. Taylor, Percy Woodfall. The vicar of St Katherine's, in the village of Strudhoe, near Lewes.

Madeleine breathed: 'That's it! That's him! He's still alive!'

I looked up, and called to the lady librarian: 'Excuse me, ma'am. Can you tell me where Lewes is? Is it near to here?'

She huffed and sniffed and looked at me as if I was

mentally defective. 'It's eight miles up the road. You can't miss it. It has a ruined castle.'

'And Strudhoe.'

'Well, oh dear, that's even closer. Three miles along the Lewes road, on the right. Between the main road and the river.'

I turned to Madeleine and I guess I was as pale as she was. If the Reverend Taylor lived that close, and if he knew where the twelve brother devils of Elmek were, then we could have this whole grotesque business finished by tonight.

CHAPTER FOUR

In winter, the valley of the Sussex Ouse is grey with mist, and you can hardly see the long backs of the Downs that surround it on both sides. At the head of the valley, you can make out the cluttered rooftops of Lewes, with its dark tumble-down castle, and from there the river Ouse flows indifferent and colourless between raised banks, sliding towards the sea. As we drove out of Newhaven and headed north along the west bank of the river, it was almost too dusky to see anything, but we could make out blotted clumps of trees, and patches of half-melted snow on the fields.

I kept the window of the car open. The English countryside in winter has a distinctive flat smell to it, mingled with the sharp aroma of woodsmoke from log fires; whereas French fields always smell of dung and frost. Madeleine strained her eyes to catch the road-sign for Strudhoe, and kept reminding me nervously to drive on the left. In the back, the copper-and-lead chest rattled softly and ominously against the side of the car as we bounced over the twisting roads.

'There!' said Madeleine. 'That's it! Next on the right!'

I saw the sign flash past in the light of my yellow French headlamps, and I put on the brakes. The turning was almost hidden by overhanging branches and narrow flint walls, and when I negotiated the Citroën across the main road and down towards the village, I felt as if we were disappearing down a rabbit-hole.

We drove slowly past whitewashed houses with ancient clay-tile roofs; tiny walled gardens and narrow brick pavements. The village was only twenty or thirty houses, all of them hundreds of years old, and I almost drove right through it and down to the fields before I realised that we'd arrived. I stopped the car, and pulled on the handbrake.

Madeleine said, 'I wonder where the vicarage is.'

'I don't know. I guess it's going to be easier to get out and look for it on foot.'

She reached over and held my hand tightly. 'Oh, God, Dan, I'm scared.'

I switched off the engine. It was only then that we heard the soft, subtle noises from the trunk at the back. We sat tense and silent in our seats, staring at each other in horror, and then we heard Elmek's dreadful whispering voice again.

'*We are near, aren't we?*'

I said nothing.

Elmek insisted: '*We are near, aren't we?*'

Madeleine nodded at me, encouraging me to answer, and I said in a taut, strained voice: 'Yes. Yes, we're near.'

'*You have done well. You have found the Reverend Taylor quickly. I will reward you, you know. I will give you the power to snap a man's neck, if that is what you want. Or to thrust knives and razors into a girl's sex. You'd enjoy that, wouldn't you?*'

I closed my eyes in desperation, but Madeleine squeezed my hand and whispered, 'Agree, Dan. All you have to do is agree.'

I said loudly: 'Yes, Elmek. I'd enjoy that.'

Elmek laughed. Then it said: '*Are you going to find the Reverend Taylor now? I can feel him! He's close by!*'

'Yes, we're going to find him.'

'*And you won't do anything foolish, will you? I am sure that the Reverend Taylor's house contains as many knives as Father Anton's. Just remember Antoinette. Didn't she scream! Didn't those knives and skewers hurt her!*'

I swallowed, painfully. 'Yes,' I said. 'They did. They hurt her very much.'

The devil laughed with a soft, creaking noise that made me shudder. I said: 'Come on, Madeleine. Let's go and find the Reverend Taylor,' and I opened the door of the car.

As I stepped out, Elmek whispered from out of its locked trunk: '*Remember – the sun has set. Your ring of hair no longer protects you. So tread wisely!*'

I climbed out of the car into the cold night air. There was a single street lamp by the corner of an old weatherboard house, shining dimly through a halo of fog. You could tell we were close to a river by the bone-chilling cold, and an almost imperceptible movement in the air, as if ghosts were brushing past us, unseen and unheeded. I coughed.

Together, we walked up the sloping street. We looked right and left, but the village was deserted. Far away, across the other side of the river, we heard a train clattering towards Newhaven, and for a moment we saw the lights of its windows through the trees.

Madeleine said, 'Dan – there's a sign here.'

I peered through the fog. On one of the old flint walls, there was a white-painted notice reading 'St Katherine's Church & Vicarage'. It pointed uphill into the gloom. I turned back for a moment and looked at our Citroën, parked at an angle beside a low hedge, and then I said: 'All right, then. We'd better see if the Reverend Taylor's at home.'

My mouth felt as if I was chewing furry caterpillars. I reached out for Madeleine's hand, and we walked as slowly as we could, but it only took a few steps before St Katherine's came into view around the houses – an ancient steepled church with a moss-covered lych-gate and a graveyard of leaning headstones. Close beside it, its windows warmly lit, was a Queen Anne vicarage, fronted with shiny blue-black bricks. There was a white porch trailed with leafless creeper, and an imposing black front door, as glossy as a coffin.

We walked across the street and approached the porch as quietly as we could. It somehow seemed sacrilegious to march around this silent fog-bound English village talking in strident voices. Madeleine leaned forward to read the engraved brass plaque on the door, and whispered: 'There it is, Dan. The Reverend P. Woodfall Taylor.'

I pulled her closer, and kissed her cheek. She smelled of French perfume and soap. She said: 'Your nose is cold.' Then I lifted the weighty brass knocker and struck it twice. Across the road, someone switched on a bedroom light.

Inside the vicarage, I heard doors opening and closing. Then the sound of someone walking towards the door. A key was turned in the lock, and then a slice of light fell across the path, and an elderly face appeared at the crack in the doorway.

'Yes?'

I said, uncertainly: 'Are you the Reverend Taylor, sir?'

'That's correct. Did you want to see me?'

I coughed. 'I'm sorry to disturb you, sir. But there's something I have to discuss.'

The old man looked at me suspiciously. He had a crest of wiry white hair, and that ruddy, well-polished face that always makes me think of English clergy as a boxful of Carolina apples. He was wearing a clerical collar and carpet slippers, and a pair of shiny grey pants that looked as if he'd pressed them under the mattress. There were deep indentations at the side of his nose where he usually wore spectacles, and that was probably why his pale, bulging eyes were regarding me so fixedly.

'You're American, aren't you?' the vicar asked, in precise tones. He even pronounced 'aren't' as 'ah-runt'. He said: 'You're not from the Mormons? Because I'm afraid I have nothing to say to the Mormons.'

'I'm not a Mormon, sir.'

'They're a terrible pest, you know. And all this ridiculous nonsense about Moroni and Boroni.'

Madeleine said, 'We've come about the tank.'

The vicar swivelled his jowly head in his stiff clerical collar and blinked at her. 'The *tank*? How very odd.'

'Why is it odd?' I asked him. I wondered if he, like Eloise, had felt some kind of premonition or psychic wave.

'Well,' said the Reverend Woodfall Taylor, 'they only came around to empty it on Tuesday.'

I stared at him uncomprehendingly and he stared back at me.

'The septic tank,' he explained. 'Isn't that what you meant?'

If I hadn't felt so sick and serious about Elmek, I think I could have laughed. But all I could say was: 'Not *that* tank, sir. The tank you once said prayers over in Normandy, during the war.'

His mouth slowly opened, as if some strong invisible hand was pulling his jaw down. He said, perplexed: '*Normandy*? The tank in *Normandy*?'

I nodded. 'It's been opened, Mr Taylor. The devil's got out.'

He stared at me in absolute slow-motion horror. Then he opened the door wide, and almost dragged us both into his cluttered little hall, among the crowded umbrella-stand and grandfather clock and coat-rack hung with ecclesiastical raincoats and hats. He slammed the door behind us, and locked it.

'You'd better come through,' he said worriedly, and ushered us into his sitting-room. 'My wife is out tonight, organising a beetle-drive for the women's institute, and that's probably just as well.'

The sitting-room smelled of pipe-smoke and logs. There was a wide open hearth, in front of which toasted a marmalade cat and three shabby armchairs. One wall of the room was lined with books like *With Net And Specimen Jar In Lahore* and *The Way Of Christ Vol. IX*, and on the chimney-breast was a muddy oil painting of the Sussex Downs at Fulking. The Reverend Taylor said: 'Sit down, please, sit down. Perhaps I can get my woman to make you a cup of coffee. Or there's whisky, if you prefer.'

'A whisky would be wonderful,' I told him. 'We came all the way over from France this morning.'

The vicar went to an antique sideboard and took out three ill-matched glasses. He filled each with neat Vat 69, and brought them over to the fireside with trembling hands. He swallowed his where he stood, wiped his mouth with a crumpled handkerchief, and said. 'Cheers.'

Madeleine said: 'We're looking for your help, Mr Taylor. We know something about the devil, but not much. Ever since the war, it's had a terrible effect on our village.'

'Oh, dear,' said the Reverend Taylor. 'I told them this business would come to a bad end. I told them a hundred times. But oh no, they never listened. You do *your* part, they said, and we'll take care of *ours*.'

'Who were *they*?' I asked him.

The Reverend Taylor looked at me in surprise. 'My dear fellow, I couldn't possibly tell you that. Quite out of the question. I was bound by the Official Secrets Act, and unless I hear to the contrary, I still am.'

'Mr Taylor,' I told him, 'I don't like to sound offensive, but this young lady and I are both in serious danger because of that tank, and I'm afraid the Official Secrets Act is going to have to go where the monkey put his nuts.'

There was a silence. A log in the crackling fire shifted and dropped, and a shower of sparks flew up the chimney.

The Reverend Taylor said: 'I'm afraid I've never really understood that expression.'

Madeleine leaned forward intently. 'Mr Taylor, she said, 'you have to help us. The devil is threatening to kill us both, unless we help it to find its brethren

'It's name is Elmek,' I said quietly. 'The devil of sharp knives and cuts. If we don't bring all thirteen devils together again, it has promised us the worst death that anyone could think of.'

The vicar sat back in his chair. His eyes went from Madeleine to me and back again. Then he said: 'You know about it, don't you? You know about it already.'

'Only some of it. Just a few fragments of information we managed to get together in France, and some good guesswork by Father Anton.'

'Father Anton!' said the Reverend Taylor, brightening. 'I had no idea that he was still alive! I'm amazed! How is he? He was so kind to me during the war, you know. A real gentleman of the cloth.'

'Father Anton died last night, Mr Taylor. He was killed when Elmek got loose.'

The Reverend Taylor dropped his gaze. 'Oh,' he said quietly. 'I'm very sorry.'

I said: 'Mr Taylor, more people are going to get hurt unless you can tell us about these devils. Father Anton said they were probably the thirteen devils that terrorised Rouen in 1045. They were exorcised by Cornelius Prelati, and sewn into sacks, but that was all he could discover.'

The Reverend Taylor sadly blew his nose. 'He was a clever man, Father Anton. Yes, he was absolutely right. They were the thirteen devils of Rouen. *Les treize diables de Rouen.*'

'But how did they get into American tanks?' asked Madeleine. 'I don't understand it at all.'

The vicar shrugged. 'I understood very little of it myself. It all happened a long time ago, when I was a very enthusiastic young vicar, and I had just been appointed to my first church in Sussex.'

'Can you tell us about it?' I asked. 'We'll keep it to ourselves, you know, if you're really worried about the Official Secrets Act.'

The Reverend Taylor looked up at me. 'Well,' he said, 'I suppose there's no harm, since you already know so much about it. Would you care for some more whisky? No? Well, I'll have one.'

We waited in silence while the vicar poured himself another drink. Then he came over and sat by the fire, and stared into the red-hot caverns of logs and branches, a man remembering hell.

'What you have to know about this part of Sussex,' he said, 'was that it bore the brunt of the Norman invasion by William the Conqueror in 1066. All this valley was occupied, and Lewes became the seat of William de Warrenne, who was one of William the Conqueror's most trusted officers. The castle at Lewes was built by de Warrenne, and on the southern slopes of the town an immense Priory was constructed, one of the largest ecclesiastical buildings ever erected in England. In its time, it was even greater than Canterbury Cathedral.'

The Reverend Taylor swallowed half a glass of whisky, and patted his lips with the back of his sleeve.

'Of course, when Henry VIII broke with Rome, the Priory was dissolved, and most of its stones were pilfered by local people to build houses. But the Priory kept some of its secrets for many centuries afterwards. It was only when Victorian railway engineers came to excavate the site where the Priory had stood, to build a line to Brighton, that they came across several remarkable things.'

I looked up at the clock on the Reverend Taylor's mantelpiece. Eight o'clock. I wondered how long Elmek would stay patient in his medieval trunk. Madeleine touched my hand, and I knew she was thinking the same thing.

The Reverend Taylor said: 'First of all, they found the tomb of William de Warrenne's wife, Gundrada, whose burial place was unknown until then. This discovery was well-publicised. But there was another find, which wasn't publicised at all. As they dug deeper, they found a sealed vault, chiselled deep into the chalk, and this contained thirteen ancient sacks of bones.'

Madeleine whispered: 'The thirteen devils.'

'Precisely,' the vicar nodded. 'The thirteen devils, the disciples of Adramelech. And according to words engraved on the lid of the vault, they had been brought across the Channel from Rouen by William de Warrenne as devils of war, concealed in strange suits of armour. He had unleashed them at Senlac, the field on which the Battle of Hastings was fought, and they had flown on Harold and his English soldiers with such ferocity that the battle was won in a matter of hours.'

The Reverend Taylor turned to me, his ruddy face made redder by the heat from the fire.

'I expect you know the story that William's archers fired their arrows into the air, so that they landed amongst the English. Well, they were not arrows, but devils; and the thing that tore out Harold's eyes was a beast from hell.'

I took out a cigarette, my first for a whole day, and lit it. I asked the Reverend Taylor: 'That was nine hundred years ago, wasn't it? How did *you* get involved?'

He looked up. 'My oldest church records showed that William de Warrenne had somehow struck a bargain with the devils. If the devils helped the Normans conquer England, he would give them his wife Gundrada as a sacrifice to Adramelech. That's why the devils came to Lewes, and that's why Gundrada died when she did. But there were powerful French exorcists at the Priory, and they managed to quell the evil spirits, and sew them up again in sacks. It was only when the railway engineers opened up the vault that they saw the light of day once more.'

'What happened to them then?'

The Reverend Taylor finished his whisky. 'They were taken to what are now the vaults of St Thaddeus, by night, and sealed away by seven Roman Catholic priests.

This, apparently, was what it took to keep them from breaking out.'

I whispered: 'Father Anton tried to seal the devil away on his own. My God, if only we'd found this out earlier.'

'A single priest would not have sufficient power,' said the Reverend Taylor. 'It had to be seven, and they had to invoke seraphim to help them. The thirteen devils of Adramelech were not to be played with.'

'And then what?' asked Madeleine. 'How did the Americans find out about them?'

'I was never really sure, my dear,' answered the vicar. 'I found out the story myself, and I wrote a short article about it in my parish magazine, in 1938. I can't imagine that my little publication ever reached as far as Washington, but some very mysterious American gentlemen got in touch with me in 1943, and asked me a great many questions about the devils and the vaults and what could be done to control them.'

'And you told them?' I asked.

'I told them all I knew, which wasn't very much. I didn't think about it for a while, but in January, 1944, I received a letter from Bishop Angmering, saying that Allied forces had a patriotic interest in the devils of Rouen, and that I was to give them every co-operation possible.'

The Reverend Taylor was obviously disturbed by his memories. He got up from his chair, and began to walk up and down the worn carpet of his sitting-room, his hands clasped firmly behind his back.

'They came one day with Roman Catholic priests, and they took the thirteen sacks away. I didn't know where they were taking them, but I begged them to be careful. I said the devils were not to be meddled with, but they said that they were quite aware of that, and that was why they wanted them.'

He sat down again, and rubbed his eyes with his knuckles.

'The next I knew, I was ordered to go to Southampton, and report to an American colonel called Sparks. He was a very brusque man, I remember. Very crisp. He said that my devils were to be used by the American forces for a secret mission. A special division. They had been brought back to life by the conjurations of the Kabbalah, and they had been promised great rewards if they fought on the side of the Allies against the Hun. I never found out what these great rewards were, but I suspect now that they may have involved . . . well, human sacrifices. I asked one of the American officers, but all he ever did was smile, and tell me that what they were doing was for western liberty and freedom.'

'So you went across to France with this division?' I asked the Reverend Taylor.

'I did, although I was kept in the rear most of the time. Since it was impracticable to take seven Roman Catholic priests along with us, it was my duty to make sure the devils stayed in their tanks, and I did this with silver crosses that had been blessed by seven priests, and with incantations from the holy exorcism. I was only required once, as you know, when one of the tanks broke a track, and they found it impossible to move.'

Madeleine slowly shook her head. 'Didn't it ever occur to you, Mr Taylor, that the devil you left in that tank would bring misery to all who lived near it?'

The Reverend Taylor frowned. 'I sealed it away . . . and they told me the tank would last for ever.'

'But, out of all the thirteen devils, this was the only devil who hadn't been rewarded, right?' I asked him.

'I suppose so.'

'So it was bound to be troublesome, and dissatisfied?'

'Well, yes.'

I sat back, and wearily ran my fingers through my hair. 'What you did, Mr Taylor, left a thirty-year plague on that community. Milk went sour, eggs went rotten, and now the devil's got out, and two people have died. Three, if you count this young lady's mother.'

The vicar licked his lips in embarrassment. He said, in a low voice: 'Is there anything I can do to help? Anything to protect you, or assist you?'

'You can tell us where the other twelve devils are.'

The Reverend Taylor blinked at me. 'The other twelve? But I haven't the faintest idea. They took them away after the war, and I never found out what happened to them. I suppose they sealed them away, once they had had their rewards, and took them off to America.'

'America? You have to be kidding! We have a devil out there who's—'

The Reverend Taylor's eyes bulged. 'You have it *out there*? You have Elmek outside my house?'

I took a deep breath. I hadn't really meant to tell him straight away. But I said, in the most controlled voice I could muster: 'I have him locked in a lead trunk, in the back of my car. He forced us to bring him to England, on pain of death by cutting or slicing or whatever it is he does. He wants to join his brethren.'

The vicar was so flustered that he got out of his chair, and then sat down again straight away. 'My dear man,' he said, breathlessly, 'do you have any notion how dangerous that creature is?'

'I saw it kill Father Anton's housekeeper, and I saw what it did to Father Anton.'

'My God,' said the Reverend Taylor, 'that was why the Americans wanted them. They're devils of war – devils of violence. Thirteen devils in army tanks were as vicious and terrible as three divisions of ordinary troops. They swept through the hills of the Suisse Normande in a matter of days. The Germans just couldn't stop them. I wasn't right up at the front line, so I never saw what they did first hand, but I heard dreadful stories from some of the German prisoners-of-war. Some of the Hun were dying of leprosy and beriberi. Tropical diseases, in northern France! Some were blazing like torches. And others were drowning in their own blood, without any apparent signs of external injury. It was a terrible business, and I was glad when Patton stopped it.'

'Why *did* he stop it?' asked Madeleine.

The Reverend Taylor pulled a face. 'Once he'd broken through Normandy, I think he felt it would be more discreet, with regard to future war trials, if his tanks didn't leave behind them the bodies of men who had died in unnatural and unholy ways.'

I took a deep drag on my cigarette. 'What I can't understand is why the church was so ready to go along with it. These devils are *enemies* of the church, aren't they?'

'People's standards are different in time of war,' said the vicar. 'I believe that the Bishop felt he was doing the right thing. And after all, the Americans did agree to take the devils away after it was all over, and dispose of them. We were all glad of that.'

I sighed, tiredly. 'But you've no idea *where* they were taken, or who took them?'

The vicar said: 'I know that Colonel Sparks took care of them once they were shipped back to England. But where he took them, or how, I was never told. It was an extremely hush-hush operation. If any inkling had leaked out – well, there would have been a terrible flap.'

Madeleine asked: 'They were brought back to England? They weren't shipped direct to America from France?'

'No, they weren't. The last time I saw them myself was at Southampton, when they were unloading them from ships. The usual dockers were told to keep well away.'

'So what makes you think they took them off to America? Couldn't they still be here?'

The Reverend Taylor scratched his head. 'I suppose so. There's only one way to find out.'

'What's that?'

'Well, you'd have to talk to Colonel Sparks himself. He always sends me a Christmas card, every year, although we never met after the war. I have his address somewhere.'

Madeleine and I exchanged anxious glances as the Reverend Taylor went across to his desk and started sorting through stacks of untidy papers in search of the American colonel's greetings cards. It was now eight-twenty, and I began to have a fearful, restless feeling that Elmek wasn't going to give us much more time. The Reverend Taylor said: 'I was sure they were here, you know. I never throw anything away.'

I took out another cigarette, and I was just about to lift it to my lips when Madeleine said: 'Dan – look. Your hand.'

I couldn't think what she was talking about at first, but then I looked down at the cigarette I was holding and saw that it was soaked pink with blood. I had a small deep cut on the end of my finger.

'It's Elmek,' said Madeleine, in a tight, desperate voice. 'Oh God, Dan, he's warning us.'

Tugging out my handkerchief, I bound up the end of my finger as best I could, but it didn't take long before the thin cotton was drenched. I said: 'Mr Taylor – I'd really appreciate it if you hurried.'

'Sorry – did you say something?' asked the vicar, looking up from his papers.

'Please hurry. I think Elmek's getting impatient.'

The Reverend Taylor shuffled through some more papers, and then he said: 'Ah – here we are! This is last year's card, so I expect he's still living there.'

He passed over the Christmas card, and Madeleine opened it up. Almost immediately, uncannily, my finger stopped bleeding, and the wound closed up. I was left with a crimson handkerchief and no visible scar at all.

The Reverend Taylor said: 'My dear chap, have you cut yourself?'

*

The transatlantic line to Silver Spring, Maryland, was crackling and faint. It was just after lunch in the States, and Mr Sparks, onetime colonel, was out mowing his lawn. His cleaning lady dithered and fussed, but eventually agreed to get him on the line. I was glad I wasn't paying the Reverend Taylor's telephone bill that quarter.

At last, a sharp voice said: 'Hello? Who is this?'

Madeleine watched me as I answered: 'I'm sorry to trouble you, sir. My name's Dan McCook, and I'm standing right now in the home of the Reverend Woodfall Taylor.'

'Oh, really? Well, that's a surprise! I haven't seen Mr Taylor since 1945. Is he well? You're not calling to tell me he's passed away, are you?'

'No, no, nothing like that. Mr Taylor's in fine shape. But I am ringing about that little business you and he were involved in on D-Day.'

There was a crackly silence.

'Can you hear me okay?' I asked him.

'Sure, I hear you. What do you know about that?'

'Well, sir, I guess I know almost everything.'

'I see. It's a Pentagon secret, I hope you realise.'

'Yes, sir, I do. But right now we need some help.'

'Help? What kind of help?'

My hand suddenly began to feel sticky on the telephone receiver. I was bleeding again, from cuts all over my hands, and the blood was running down my sleeve. Madeleine said: 'Oh Dan, tell him to *hurry*. Elmek will kill you!'

I whispered, 'Okay, okay – the cuts aren't bad. He's just trying to needle me.'

Mr Sparks said: 'Are you there? Are you still there?'

'Yes, Mr Sparks, sorry. Listen, I need to know where the twelve remaining sacks were taken. You left one behind in Normandy. Where are the rest? Were they shipped to the States? Or were they left in England?'

There was another silence. Then Mr Sparks said: 'Well . . . I'm not sure I'm allowed to tell you that.'

'Mr Sparks, please. It's a matter of life or death. That devil you left behind in Normandy has got out of its tank. We have to find the rest of them.'

'Well, Mr McCook, we called them ANPs, which was short for Assisting Non-Military Personnel. We certainly never knew them as, well, devils. They were ANPs.'

'All right, Mr Sparks. ANPs. But where were they taken? Are they hidden in the States?'

'No, they aren't,' said Mr Sparks, reluctantly. 'They were shipped back to England, and put into cold storage, militarily speaking. I believe that General Eisenhower wanted them taken back to the States, but the problems of carrying them over and keeping them under lock and key were too tricky right then. We knew very little about them, and so we left them where they were.'

'And where was that?'

'Well, we wanted to take them back to St Thaddeus, where they originally came from. But we'd made a deal with the Bishop that we would take them off his hands. So we transported them to London, and they were sealed up in a house that belonged to the British War Office.'

'You mean they're still there? Now?'

'As far as I know. I've never heard any news to the contrary.'

The blood was beginning to dry on the back of my hand. Madeleine was staring at me anxiously, and through the door I could see the Reverend Taylor, pouring himself another Scotch. I can't say that I blamed him.

I said hoarsely: 'Mr Sparks, do you know where the house is? Even roughly?'

'Why sure. Eighteen Huntington Place, just off the Cromwell Road.'

'Are you sure?'

'Sure I'm sure. I had to go there four or five times.'

I leaned back against the brown flowers of the Reverend Taylor's wallpaper, and closed my eyes.

'Mr Sparks,' I said, 'I don't know how to thank you.'

'Don't bother. I shouldn't be telling you anyway.'

'If we get out of this alive,' I told him, 'I'll pay you a personal visit and bring you a bottle of brandy.'

There was a long pause. I could hear another faint voice on a crossed line. Then ex-Colonel Sparks said: 'What do you mean – if you come out of this alive?'

I didn't know what to answer. I just set down the telephone receiver and said to Madeleine: 'He knew where they were. We're going to have to drive to London.'

The Reverend Taylor came out to the hall and his face was even more flushed than ever. 'Are you sure you won't have another drink?' he asked us. 'Or how about some sandwiches? My woman's going home in a moment, but she could rustle up some tongue sandwiches.'

'Really,' I said, 'that's very kind of you, but we have to go right away.'

The vicar looked at me nervously. 'Did Colonel Sparks know where they were? Did he tell you?'

I nodded. 'He knew where they were sealed away after the war. Whether they're still there or not is another matter. But we're going to have to go to find out.'

'Oh, dear,' said the Reverend Taylor, 'this is all very distressing. I told them it would come to a bad end.'

Madeleine said: 'It wasn't your fault, Mr Taylor. You weren't to know.'

'But I feel dreadfully responsible,' he told us worriedly. 'I feel as if it was my negligence that killed poor Father Anton.'

'Well, maybe you can make up for it, I suggested. 'Maybe you can give us some idea of how to protect ourselves against these thirteen devils and against Adramelech.'

The Reverend Taylor's face fell. 'My dear fellow, I hardly know what to say. It was only because we had such a great number of priests during the war that we were able to keep the devils under control. But as for Andramelech himself – well, I'm afraid I don't know what to tell you. Adramalech is one of the greatest and most terrible of the evil Sephiroth. Perhaps only one of the *divine* Sephiroth would be able to help you, and according to what is written about them, the divine Sephiroth are almost as unmanageable as the evil ones. Adramelech's counterpart among God's ranks is Hod, the seraph of majesty and glory; but whether Hod could possibly be summoned to help you – well, I really couldn't say. It's all so infernally mythical.'

I lit a fresh cigarette. This time, my fingers stayed intact. Perhaps Elmek had realised that we had the information that we'd come for, and that he'd soon be rejoining his malevolent brethren.

I said: 'Do you really believe in all this? In Adramelech and Hod? And all these devils. I never knew the Protestant church held with devils.'

The Reverend Taylor stuck his hands in his pockets and looked a little abashed.

'You will rarely find a Protestant cleric who admits to the actual physical existence of devils,' he said. 'But every Anglican priest is told in strict confidence of the evidence that exists to support them. I couldn't possibly divulge what the books say, but I assure you that the evidence I have personally seen for the existence of the divine and the evil Sephiroth is more than overwhelming. There are demons and devils, Mr McCook, just as there are angels.'

Just then, I felt a low-frequency vibration tremble through the house. It was like a sinister train passing, a train that blew a deep dark whistle. I looked up at the ceiling, and I saw a hairline crack that ran all the way from one plaster moulding to the other.

The Reverend Taylor looked up, too. 'What on earth's that?' he blinked. 'Did you feel it?'

'Yes, I felt it,' said Madeleine. 'Maybe it was a supersonic plane passing.'

The Reverend Taylor frowned. 'I don't think Concorde flies this way, my dear. But I suppose it could—'

There was another rumble, louder this time. The floors shook and a fiery log dropped out of the grate and into the hearth. The Reverend Taylor hurriedly unhooked the tongs from the firedog, and stacked the log back on the fire.

I said: 'It's Elmek. I'm sure of it. He's restless. Come on, Madeleine, I think we ought to get out of here before anything worse happens.'

The Reverend Taylor raised his hand. 'You mustn't leave on my account. I was just as responsible for what happened as anybody. And perhaps I can help.'

He went across to his bookshelves, and spent three or four minutes searching for what he wanted. He tugged it out at last — a small book as thin as a New Testament, with black leather covers and a frayed silk bookmark. Holding the book longsightedly at arm's length, he licked his thumb and leafed through six or seven pages. Madeleine and I waited impatiently, while the clock struck nine.

'Ah, here it is. The invocation of angels.'

'I have a French book about that in my luggage,' I told him. '*L'Invocation des Anges* by Henri St Ermin. The trouble is, I can hardly understand a word of it.'

Again, the house trembled. A china donkey with a dried-up cactus in its pannier was shaken off its shelf, and shattered on the floor. Two or three books dropped out, and the windows vibrated in their frames with a sound that set my teeth on edge.

'*L'Invocation des Anges* is just what you need,' said the Reverend Taylor, a little breathless. 'But this book will help you identify each of the twelve other devils in turn and call an appropriate angel to dismiss it. Did Father Anton mention the seven tests to you?'

'You mean the seven tests of a devil's identity? Yes, he did.'

The Reverend Taylor nodded gravely. 'A brilliant man, Father Anton. I can't tell you how sorry I am that he's gone. Well, he was absolutely right. When you find the devils you must identify each in turn, and use your book *L'Invocation des Anges* to send them away. They are French devils, you see, and French dismissals will have a greater effect on them.'

Madeleine said: 'If we dismiss them, will that prevent them from summoning Adramelech?'

The Reverend Taylor looked at her seriously. 'One hopes so, my dear. But of course devils are devils, and one can never quite predict how they are going to behave, or what tricks they are going to use. Take this terrible beast Elmek, for example—'

The curtains covering the windows suddenly flapped, as if they were being blown by a wind that we couldn't even feel. I turned towards the window in fright, and I was sure that for one second I glimpsed, in the darkness outside, the evil slanting eyes of the demon of knives. Above us, the lights went dim and sickly, until we could hardly see each other, and a sour smell of decay flowed through the room.

The Reverend Taylor shivered. Then he raised his hand and drew the sign of the cross in the air, and called: 'Devil, begone! I adjure thee, O vile spirit, to go out! God the Father, in His name, leave our presence! God the Son, in His name, make thy departure! God the Holy Ghost, in His name, quit this place! Tremble and flee, O impious one, for it is—'

There was a howl so loud that I jumped in terror. It sounded as if a fearsome beast was actually devouring the whole room. The curtains lifted and flapped again, and a whole row of books toppled like dominoes and splayed across the carpet. Madeleine clutched my arm in fear, and the Reverend Taylor raised both his hands to protect himself from the rushing sound of demonic hate.

'It is God who commands thee!' shouted the Reverend Taylor. 'It is I who command thee!'

The windows burst in a cloud of tumbling, spraying, razor-sharp glass. Fragments flew across the room and hit the Reverend Taylor in a glittering explosion that sliced into his upraised hands, ripped the ecclesiastical cloth from his arms and chest, and slashed his face and hands right down to the raw nerves. Before he collapsed, I saw the whiteness of his forearm bones, laid bare amidst the chopped meat of his flesh.

Miraculously, or devilishly, the glass passed Madeleine and me and left us almost unscratched. We watched in horror as the Reverend Taylor sank to the floor, ripped into bloody pieces, and Madeleine pressed her face into my shoulder, gagging with horror.

The last fragments of glass tinkled on to the floor, and a freezing wind blew in through the window. Holding Madeleine close, I said: 'Elmek.'

There was no answer.

'*Elmek!*' I said, louder.

Outside, in the darkness, there was a dry, laughing sound. It could have been laughing or it could have been the swish of the trees as the wind moaned through their leafless branches.

The door of the sitting-room opened and I froze in fright. But then a red-faced woman in a turquoise overcoat and a turban hat peered around the door and said: 'What a commotion! Is everything all right? I thought I heard glass.'

The Sussex Constabulary kept us at Lewes Police Station for almost three hours. Most of the time, we sat on hard wooden seats in a green-painted corridor and read the same crime-prevention posters over and over. An unsmiling superintendent with a clipped black moustache and shoes that were polished beyond human reason asked us questions and examined our passports, but we knew from the start that the Reverend Taylor's hideous death could only look like an accident. A freak accident, of course. But an accident all the same.

Elmek, in his lead-and-copper trunk, was not going to be delayed or thwarted, especially by the procedures of the British police.

At five minutes to midnight, the superintendent came out of his office and handed us our passports.

'Does this mean we can go?' I asked him.

'For the moment, sir. But we'd like a forwarding address. You may have to give evidence at the inquest.'

'Well, okay. The Hilton Hotel.'

The superintendent took out a silver propelling-pencil and wrote that down. 'All right, sir. Thanks for your help. We're advising your embassy of what's happened, just as a matter of courtesy.'

'That's all right by me.'

The superintendent tucked away his pencil and regarded us for a moment with eyes that looked as if they'd been pickled in bleach. I knew that he didn't really understand how the Reverend Taylor's window had blown in with such devastating force, or how Madeleine and I had escaped with nothing but superficial cuts. But there was no sign of explosives, no sign of weapons, no motive, and no possibility that we could have cut him to shreds ourselves with thousands of fragments of glass. I had already heard one constable muttering to his sergeant about 'peculiar vacuums' and 'thousand-to-one chances', and I guessed that they were going to put the Reverend Taylor's death down to some wild peculiarity of the English weather.

'You won't be leaving the country, sir?' asked the superintendent. 'Not for a few days, anyway?'

'No, no. We'll stick around.'

'Very well, sir. That'll be all for now, sir. I'll bid you goodnight.'

We left the police station and walked across the road to the sloping car park. The Citroën, silent and dark, was the only car there. We climbed into it warily, and sat back in the rigid little seats. Madeleine yawned, and pulled her fingers through her dark blonde hair. I glanced back at the devil's chest, and said: 'If Elmek's going to let us, I think it's time we had some rest. I didn't sleep last night, and I don't suppose we're going to get ourselves a lot of relaxation tomorrow.'

There was no answer from the dull medieval box. Either the devil was sleeping itself (although I didn't know if devils slept or not) or else it was silently granting me permission to rest. I started up the car, and we went in search of somewhere to stay.

We spent half an hour driving around the streets of Lewes in the dark before Madeleine spotted a bed-and-breakfast sign on the outskirts of town, on a gateway just opposite the forbidding flint walls of Lewes prison. Set back from the road in a driveway of laurel bushes was a red-brick Victorian mansion, and someone was watching a black-and-white television in the front downstairs room. I turned the Citroën into the driveway, parked it, and went to the front door to knock.

I was answered, after a long and frosty wait, by a small hunched old woman in a pink candlewick dressing-gown and paper curlers. She said: 'It's very late, you know. Did you want a room?'

I tried my best not to look like a dishevelled madman or an escaped convict from across the road. 'If that's possible. We've come from France today and we're pretty well bushed.'

'Well, I can't charge you the full rate. You've missed three hours' sleep already.'

I looked at her in disbelief for a moment, and all I

129

could say was: 'That's okay. That's wonderful. But I'll pay the full rate if you want me to.'

I called Madeleine, and the old woman let us into the house. She took us up a cold flight of stairs to a landing laid with green-and-cream linoleum, where a painting of ducks by Peter Scott hung under a frayed and dusty lampshade. She unlocked a door for us, and showed us into a typically freezing British bedroom, with a high double bed of cream-painted iron, a cheap varnished wardrobe, a cracked sink and a gas fire with half of its fireclay missing.

'We'll take it,' I said wearily, and I sat down on the bed and took off my shoes before she could even answer. The mattress felt as if it was crowded with unravelled fencing wire, but right then it was heaven. The old lady left us alone together, and we undressed, washed in Arctic water, and fell into bed. I don't remember falling asleep, but it must have been pretty quick, because I didn't even have time to put my arm around Madeleine's naked back.

I was wakened by a scuffling noise. For a second, I wasn't sure if I was dreaming or not, but then I heard it again, and I lifted my head from the pillow and looked around. I held my breath, and tried to suppress the *pump-pump-pump* of my heart. The room was very dark, suffocatingly dark, and even though I strained my eyes, I couldn't see if there was anything there. I lifted myself up on one elbow, and the bedsprings creaked and complained like a tired orchestra.

There was silence. I whispered, though I didn't want to: 'Elmek?'

No reply. Madeleine stirred in her sleep, and turned over.

I whispered again: 'Elmek?'

There was another scuffle, then a rustling sound. They seemed to come from down behind the foot of the bed. I sat up, my skin electric with fear, and I tried to see what was hiding there in the darkness.

Again, there was silence. But I was sure I heard a faint scratching and rustling on the worn linoleum, and I was sure that a darker shadow shifted and moved in the gloom.

I kept absolutely still. I could feel that Madeleine was awake now. She reached across the bed and squeezed my hand, too frightened to speak. But I bent my head towards her and said softly: 'Don't panic. It's in here somewhere, but don't panic.'

She nodded, and swallowed. In the hush of the night, we waited for the devil to stir again, our hands tightly clenched together, our breath held back into shallow gasps.

Suddenly, Madeleine said: 'Dan. The window. *Dan!*'

I turned towards the window. I flinched in shock. There was someone silhouetted against the curtains, a tall figure of clotted shadows, unmoving and quiet. I took one look, and then my hand went scrambling in search of my bedside lamp, but I tangled my fingers in the flex by mistake, and the lamp tipped over and crashed on to the floor.

In the terrible silence that followed, a woman's voice said: '*Are you rested?*'

It was a strange, throaty voice; too deep for a woman, really, but too vibrantly female for a man. The dim figure stirred, and moved silently across the room. I could just make out a pale face – a smudge of grey in the grainy blackness.

'Who are you?' I demanded. 'Who are you?'

The figure didn't reply for a while. It seemed to be grating its teeth together, with an edgy, squeaking sound. Then it said: '*We take many forms, you know. Many substances. Aren't you afraid?*'

I said: 'Are you Elmek?'

'*Elmek or Asmorod or Kaphis. We have more names than nights* that have passed since the crucifixion. *Don't think that your book can identify us, because it won't.*'

'What do you know about that?'

The thing gave a hoarse, blowzy laugh. '*I know that you are wasting your time in religious folly. Angels! You must be demented. You have struck yourself a bargain with me, my friend, and with my master Adramelech, the Grand Chancellor of Hell, the peacock and the serpent. Don't talk to me of angels!*'

Madeleine said: 'What are you going to do with us? You're not going to keep your bargain, are you?'

There was a sound of crackling, as if the beast were tugging its knuckles, or biting into bones. Then it said, in a much deeper, more slurred and masculine voice: '*Bargains are struck for good and evil. Bargains have always been struck for good and evil. The priests and the bishops have struck bargains before, and not been disappointed. We didn't only fight at Senlac, you know. We were there with Charlemagne, and we were there with Jeanne d'Arc. No wonder the English burned her! The stories told of monstrous devils whirling around her head in battle, and they were true,* mon ami. *It is only now that the church has seen fit to rewrite its history, and deny the existence of all the unholy allies it used for its so-called holy wars!*'

Madeleine was shivering in fright. I put my arm around her and held her close, but the devil wasn't disturbed.

'*Think of the Spanish Inquisition,*' it whispered. '*Think of the torture chambers of England and France. Each had its devil! In times gone by, devils walked the earth freely, and they still walk the earth! They made bargains with men, for mutual advantage, because man is an evil creature, thank the stars, as well as a good one.*'

Over in the corner of the room, near the door, I saw a faint blueish light, like the phosphorescence in the ocean at night. Then, to my horror, something began to appear out of the darkness. I stared and stared, and, half-distinguishable in the shadows, its mouth stretched back in a wolfish grin, was a beast that could have been a

132

devil, could have been a whoreish woman, could have been some hideous slimy subaqueous squid. There was a sour smell in the room, and the blue light crawled and flickered like the foul illumination from decaying fish.

I saw everything in that moment that disgusted and horrified me. I saw what looked like a woman's hands seductively drawn back up a curving shining thigh, only to realise that the thigh wasn't a thigh at all, but a desperately wriggling trunk of tentacles. I saw pouting lips that suddenly turned out to be festering cuts. I saw rats crowding into the mouth of a sleeping woman. I saw living flesh cut away from living bones, first in ribbons of skin and muscle, and then in a stomach-turning tangle of sodden flesh.

Madeleine, beside me, shrieked.

'*Elmek!*' I yelled, and rolled out of the bed towards the ghastly apparition.

There was a paralysing burst of white light, and I felt as if someone had cracked me over the head with a pickaxe handle. Dazed and dazzled, I fell sideways on the cold lino, bruising my shoulder against the leg of the bed. I tried to get up, but something hit me again, something heavy and soft.

Madeleine screamed: 'Dan! It's in the bed! *It's in the bed!*'

Stunned, wiping blood away from a split lip, I gripped hold of the edge of the mattress and pulled myself upright. Madeleine was beating in terror at the blankets, as if something had scurried its way under them, and was crawling around her legs. For a half-second, in the eerie blue light of that failing phosphorescence, I saw something reach out from under the covers and touch her naked leg. It was black and claw-like and hairy, like a grossly overgrown spider. I hit at it, yelling in fear and anger, and then I seized Madeleine's wrist and yanked her off the bed and halfway across the floor.

There was a moment of sheer panic when I thought

133

that whatever was under those blankets was going to come crawling after us. I heard something heavy drop off the bed, and the scratch of claws on the floor; but then the blue light suddenly began to flicker again, and go dim, like a torch with used-up batteries, and the sour odour of devil began to fade away. I heard a soft soughing noise, a wind where no wind could blow, and then there was silence. Both of us crouched on the floor, panting from fright. We listened and listened, but there was no sound in the room at all, and after a while we cautiously raised our heads.

'I think it must have gone,' I said quietly.

Madeleine whispered: 'Oh God, that was terrible. Oh my God, I was so scared.'

I switched on the overhead light. Then I went over to the bed and prodded at the covers with the broken bedside lamp. In the end, I gathered up enough courage to lift the blankets and turn them over. There was nothing there. If it hadn't been a terrifying illusion, then it had left us.

Madeleine came up behind me and touched my back. 'I don't think I could sleep any more,' she told me. 'Not in that bed. Why don't we start out for London?'

I found my wristwatch where it had been knocked on the floor. It was five-thirty in the morning. It would soon be dawn.

'All right,' I said, feeling very little better than I had when we first went to bed. 'It looks like Elmek's pushing us on, in any case. Remind me to remember that devils rarely sleep.'

Madeleine put on her blue jeans without panties, and combed out her hair in front of the dingy mirror. I said: 'I can't take much more of this. I don't even know why it does these things.'

'Maybe it's boasting,' suggested Madeleine. 'They're supposed to be vain creatures, aren't they, devils?'

'It could be that. If you ask me, it's just relishing how

frightened we are. It intends to squeeze the last ounce of fear and agony out of us two and get its goddamned money's worth.'

Madeleine tugged a grey ribbed sweater over her head. It was so cold in that bedroom I could see the outline of her nipples through the thick Shetland wool. 'I don't know,' she said. 'I have the feeling it's *excited*, as if it's getting itself all worked up to join its brethren. All that boasting about what devils had done in the past. And that figure, whatever it was, with all those squids and snakes and things. That was like some horrible kind of showing-off.'

I brushed my hair, and did my best to shave with a blunt razor and no soap. There were dark smudges of tiredness under my eyes, and I looked about as nealthy as a can of week-old tuna. In fact, I was so exhausted that I could hardly feel frightened any more. When we were ready, we tiptoed out on to the landing, and went downstairs through the dark, creaking house. There was no-one around, so I left three pounds on the hall table and we let ourselves out into the freezing early morning.

The sun came up over the Sussex Downs just as we were driving out of Brighton. On each side of us, the long frosted hills stretched into the haze; to Chanctonbury Ring in the west, and to Ditchling Beacon in the east. At that time of the morning, in winter, Sussex has a strangely prehistoric feel to it, and you become uncannily sensitive to the memory that Ancient Britons trod these downs, and Roman legions, and suspect that across the smokey plain of the Sussex Weald, the fires of Anglo-Saxon ironfounders could be seen glimmering in the depths of the forests. Beside me, Madeleine sat huddled in her coat trying to doze as we turned northwards towards London

We drove along roads white with ice, past old cottages and pubs and filling stations and roadside shops advertising home-made fudge and large red potatoes. Behind us, in the back of the car, the copper-and-lead box was silent as a tomb. The sun rose on my right, and flickered behind the spare trees as I sped on to the motorway. In another hour, we would reach the suburbs of London. By noon, we would probably discover whether Elmek was going to keep his bargain or not. I thought of the saying that 'he who sups with devils must needs use a long spoon', and it didn't encourage me very much.

As we left the fields and the countryside behind, and came into the crowded grey streets of Croydon and Streatham, the sky grew ominously dark, and I had to drive with my headlamps on. On the wet sidewalks, shoppers and passers-by hurried with coat-collars turned up against the cold, and a few first flakes of snow settled on my windshield. The traffic was crowded and confused, and it took another hour of edging my way between red double-decker buses and black shiny taxis before I crossed the Thames over Chelsea Bridge, and made my way towards the Cromwell Road. The snow was falling heavily now, but it melted as soon as it touched the busy streets and pavements. I passed Sloane Square, with its fountains and bedraggled pigeons; turned left at Knightsbridge, and then juddered along in solid traffic past Harrods and the Victoria & Albert Museum. Today, London looked grimly Dickensian; and as we drove by the Natural History Museum, with its twisted Gothic pillars and its gardens arranged with petrified trees, I felt as if bringing this medieval devil into the city was part of some dark and sinister Victorian plot. Only my tiredness and my fear reminded me that what was inside that locked trunk was hideously real, and that this morning in December in London was overshadowed with the vicious horror of mankind's most ancient enemies. I lit up a cigarette, and coughed.

At last, we arrived outside 18, Huntingdon Place. It was a late-Victorian house of grimy yellow-and-grey bricks, in that gloomy hinterland between Cromwell

Road and High Street Kensington, all shared flats and registry offices and unfashionable mews. I pulled the car into the kerb, and nudged Madeleine awake. She blinked, and stretched, and said: 'Are we here already? That was the best sleep I've had in days.'

There was no sign on the black spiked railings outside the house to show that it still belonged to the Ministry of Defence. But I climbed stiffly out of the car, and walked up to the front door to see if there was any kind of identification by the two rows of doorbells. There was nothing at all, not even the name of a tenant. The door itself was firmly locked, and by the condition of its cracked grey paint, looked as if it hadn't been decorated for twenty years. I tried to peer through a dirty pane of spiderweb glass beside it, but inside the house it was completely dark.

Madeleine came across the sidewalk. 'Any luck?' she asked me.

'I don't know. It looks as if it's empty. Maybe they just shut the devils up here and left it.'

'But that was thirty years ago.'

I shrugged. 'We could always ring the bell and see.'

I looked back towards the Citroën, parked against the kerb in the softly-falling snow. 'We have to get in here somehow,' I told her. 'Otherwise it's going to be cold cuts for lunch.'

'Maybe the next-door neighbours know something,' she suggested. 'Even if the house is empty, it must belong to somebody. If we could only get ourselves a key, and take a look round. We could always pretend we wanted to buy it.'

I stepped back and looked up at the second and third floors of the house, blinking against the snow that fell in my upturned face. 'I can't see any lights. I guess it must be empty '

I went back up to the porch and pushed all the bells. I could hear some of them ringing in different parts of the house. Then I waited for a while, shuffling my feet to bring the circulation back to my toes. Madeleine looked at me tiredly, and I knew that both of us were pretty close to the end of our tether. A taxi drove by, blowing its horn.

We were just about to turn away when we heard a noise inside the house. I raised my eyes in surprise. Then there were sharp footsteps coming along the corridor, the rattle of security chains, and the door opened. A lean young man in a black jacket and grey business pants stood there, with a haughty and enquiring expression on his face.

'Did you want something?' he asked, in that clipped voice that immediately told you he'd been given a superior education and probably read *Horse & Hound*.

I gave him an uneasy kind of a smile. 'I'm not sure,' I told him. 'Does this building still belong to the War Office?'

'You mean the Ministry of Defence.'

'That's right. I mean the Ministry of Defence.'

The young man looked sour. 'Well, that depends who you are and why you wish to know.'

'Then it does?'

The young man looked even sourer.

I said: 'The reason I want to know is because I have some property that belongs to the Ministry of Defence. Part of a set of wartime equipment. And what I'm doing is bringing it back.'

'I see,' said the young man. 'And would you mind telling me what this piece of equipment might be?'

'Do you have a superior officer here?' I asked him.

He gave a patronising grimace. 'I haven't even said this is Ministry property yet.'

'Okay,' I told him. 'If it *is* Ministry property, and you *do* have a superior officer, tell him we have Adramelech's thirteenth friend. Right out here, in the back of the car.'

'I *beg* your pardon?'

'Just tell him. Adramelech's thirteenth friend. We'll wait here for five minutes.'

The young man pulled a very disconcerted face, and then he said: 'I suppose you'd better wait inside. I won't be a moment.'

He opened the door wider, and we stepped into a musty-smelling hall with an olive-green dado that was worn shiny with age. I lit another cigarette and passed one to Madeleine. She wasn't an experienced smoker, and she puffed at it like a thirteen-year-old with her first Camel, but right now we needed anything that could steady our nerves. On the peeling wall just behind us was a mildew-spotted photograph of Earl Haig, and if that wasn't an out-and-out admission that 18, Huntingdon Place belonged to the Ministry of Defence, I don't know what could have been, apart from a tank parked outside.

I took out my handkerchief and blew my nose. What with losing two nights of sleep, and chasing around in the bitter winter weather, I was beginning to show all the symptoms of a headcold. Madeleine leaned tiredly against the wall beside me, and looked too drained to say anything.

After a few minutes, I heard voices on the upstairs landing, and then an immaculately-creased pair of khaki trousers came into view down the stairs, followed by a crisp khaki jacket with a Sam Browne belt and medal ribbons, and then a fit, square face with a bristling white moustache and the kind of eyes that were crowsfooted from peering across the horizons of the British Empire.

The officer came forward with a brisk, humourless smile. He said: 'They didn't give me your names, unfortunately. Remiss of them.'

I flipped my cigarette out into the snow. 'I'm Dan McCook, this is Madeleine Passerelle.'

The officer gave a sharp, brief nod of his head, as if he were trying to shake his eyebrows loose. 'I'm Lieutenant-Colonel Thanet, Special Operations Branch.'

There was a silence. He was obviously expecting us to explain why we were here. I looked at Madeleine and Madeleine looked back at me.

Lieutenant-Colonel Thanet said: 'They tell me you have something interesting. Something that belongs to us.'

'I guess it does in a way,' I told him.

He gave a tight, puckered smiled. The kind of smile that my grandfather, who came from Madison, Wisconsin, used to describe as 'a close view of a mule's ass.' He said: 'Something to do with D-Day, if I understand correctly.'

I nodded. 'You can threaten us with the Official Secrets Act if you want to, but we know what happened anyway, so I don't think there's much point. We know about the thirteen ANPs that you British loaned to Patton, and we know what happened to them afterwards. Twelve of them came here, and were sealed up, and the thirteenth one was left in a tank in Normandy, and conveniently forgotten. What we have out here, in the back of our car, is your thirteenth ANP.'

The colonel looked at me with those clear, penetrating eyes. I could see that he was trying to work out what kind of a johnny I was, and what official category this particular problem fitted into, and what the correct follow-up procedure was going to be.

But what he said wasn't army jargon, and he didn't say it like a man whose decisions are usually taken by the letter of the military rulebook. He said: 'Are you telling me the truth, Mr McCook? Because if you are, then I'm very seriously worried.'

I pushed the door wider so that he could see the Citroën parked at the kerb. 'It's in the trunk,' I told him. 'And it's the real thing. Its name is Elmek, or Asmorod. The devil of knives and sharpness.'

He bit his lip. He was silent for a while, and then he

said: 'Is it safe? I mean, is it sealed up, in any religious way?'

I shook my head.

The colonel asked: 'Do you know anything about it? Anything about it at all?'

'Yes. It told us it was a disciple of Adramelech, the Grand Chancellor of Hell. We took it out of the tank in France because it was disturbing the people who lived near it, and because Mlle Passerelle believed it was responsible for killing her mother. But since then, it's killed three other people, and it's threatened to do the same to us.'

Madeleine said to the colonel: '*Monsieur le colonel*, you don't seem at all incredulous. I would even say that you believed us.'

The colonel managed a twisted little grin. 'It's hardly surprising, *mademoiselle*. It has been my particular brief for the last six years to look into that ANP business after D-Day. I probably know more about that special division of tanks than anybody alive.'

'Then it's true?' I asked him. 'The other devils are really here?'

'Who told you that?'

'An American gentleman named Sparks. He was one of the people involved in the special division during the war.'

Lieutenant-Colonel Thanet sighed, as if he expected that kind of behaviour from Americans.

'Is it true?' I questioned him. 'Are they really here?'

Thanet said: 'Yes. They're sealed in the cellars. All twelve of them. It's been part of my job to work out a way of using them again.'

'Using them again? Wasn't once enough?'

'Probably. But you know what departments of defence are like. Anything cheap and unusual and lethal always appeals to their sense of humour. And these days, they particularly like nasty alternatives to nuclear weaponry.

So they dug out the file on the ANPs, and sent me here to see what I could do.'

'And have you done anything?' asked Madeleine.

'Not much so far. We've had a couple of beggars out of their sacks and had a look at their bones and their general physiology, and we know that as long as their seal is broken, they can take on flesh again, and live. That was how it was done in World War Two, and that's why we haven't broken any of the seals. But we're planning on greater things, once we're sure we can keep them under control.'

'Greater things?' I queried. 'What does that mean?'

'Well,' said the colonel, with a furrowed frown, 'we were going to try to conjure up their master, because he's supposed to be several thousand times more powerful.'

'*Adramelech?*' breathed Madeleine, her eyes wide.

'That's right. The great and terrible Samarian deity. Well, I wouldn't have believed it back when I was at Sandhurst, but once they showed me what that special division had done under Patton . . .'

He looked at me with a meaningful inclination of his cropped and white-haired head.

'There were photographs taken after D-Day, you know,' he told us. 'Photographs and even colour films. They were quite extraordinary. I should think that, apart from the H-Bomb, they're unquestionably the most spectacular and most secret things that NATO have got.'

I said: 'How can we control something like Adramelech, when we can hardly control these thirteen devils of his?'

Lieutenant-Colonel Thanet rubbed the back of his neck. 'Well, that's a tricky one, and that's why I'm rather worried that you've brought our friend Elmek over. We *don't* know how to control these devils for certain, and we certainly have no idea what to do with Adramelech. We don't even know what Adramelech could possibly look like, and that's always supposing one could actually see

142

such a thing with the human eye. One way we've kept the situation under control is by leaving the thirteenth devil where it was, in France. Oh yes, we knew it was there. But we wanted to leave it there, at least until we worked out a foolproof way to prevent these other twelve beggars from setting fire to us, or giving us leprosy, or strangling us with our own guts.'

I reached out for Madeleine's hand. Her fingers were very cold when I touched them.

'Now they're all back together, of course, there's a definite risk that they'll summon up their master,' said Thanet. 'Patton's men prevented such a thing from happening during the war because they promised Adramelech some human sacrifices, and plenty of blood. One could do such a thing in wartime. But now, well . . . the only blood that's immediately available is ours.'

I took out another cigarette, and lit it. Outside the door, the snow had stopped falling, but the sky was still a grim metallic green. The Citroën stood silently by the kerb, and through the reflecting glass of the rear window, we could just make out the side of the copper-and-lead trunk.

'I was afraid of that, too,' I said hoarsely, and Madeleine looked away with an expression of such sadness that even Lieutenant-Colonel Thanet noticed it, and half-raised his hand to comfort her.

CHAPTER FIVE

They gave us a in Lieutenant-Colonel Thanet's upstairs office, and we sat on uncomfortable folding chairs while he took out his files on the special division of tanks – codename *Stripes*. He leafed through them with the quick, concentrated frown of a speed-reader, pausing now and then to study a chart or a graph, and to glance up at Madeleine and me and give a swift apologetic *moue* for the time he was taking.

The office was cold, and the pale-blue walls with their defence maps of Britain and Western Europe made it seem even colder. A radiator the size of a small pig rattled and steamed in one corner, but it was all noise and no heat. There were three khaki tin filing cabinets on the opposite wall, and these, apart from Lieutenant-Colonel Thanet's desk and three collapsible chairs, were the only furniture.

I stood up and took my cup of scalding tea across to the window. In the dull, glistening street below, three British Army sergeants were lifting Elmek's box from the back of the Citroën. The devil hadn't spoken a word since our arrival, but we knew the risks of ignoring it. It expected to be reunited with its twelve brethren, and if it wasn't, then God help any of us who were close to a window, or a knife, or anything that could cut into human flesh.

Lieutenant-Colonel Thanet cleared his throat, and neatly collated his files in front of him.

'Did you find anything?' I asked him.

He pulled a face. 'Not very much, I'm afraid. Not much more than I was aware of already. The whole history of this particular operation was kept under wraps, and there really isn't a great deal of documentary evidence to go on. It appears from the early approaches made by the Pentagon to the British War Office that General Patton was largely responsible for thinking it up and carrying it through, although Eisenhower certainly knew about it six or seven months before D-Day. There are several references here to Operation Stripes, and this paper here is the requisition order for preparing the tanks. Each tank cost eighteen thousand dollars to refit, mainly because of the steering mechanisms, which were partly remote-controlled.'

Madeleine said: 'Does it mention Adramelech? Does it say how they kept him under control?'

Thanet slowly shook his head. 'There's only one reference here that might be relevant. It refers to the transportation of German prisoners-of-war to England, including one French woman, a Nazi collaborator. They were taken to the army camp at Aldershot under the direct authority of Colonel Sparks – that's your American friend – and Colonel T. K. Allingham, who was his British counterpart, and that means their movement order must have had something to do with Operation Stripes. It's possible that these prisoners may have been used to appease Adramelech. Sacrifices, for want of a better word.'

'A man for each of the thirteen devils, and a woman for Adramelech himself,' Madeleine suggested quietly.

'Quite possible,' said Lieutenant-Colonel Thanet, smiling an uneasy smile. 'Your theory is as valid as anybody's. That movement order is the only written evidence of those prisoners that survives.'

I came away from the window and laid my thick-rimmed government teacup back in its saucer. 'Colonel Thanet,' I told him, 'we may have only a few hours, even a few minutes, before those thirteen devils get together and call up their master. Then what are we going to do?'

'We're not going to panic, and that's for certain,' said the colonel. 'First of all, we're going to make quite sure that the devils' religious seals are quite intact, because there isn't much they can do while they're nothing more than exorcised bags of bones.'

'Supposing Elmek can free them – bring them back to life?'

'It would have to be a pretty powerful kind of devil to do that. Each one of those seals has been blessed by seven Roman Catholic priests and kissed by a Roman Catholic cardinal. You may be cynical about religion, but I can tell you from my own experience, that's strong medicine.'

Madeleine lowered her eyes. 'We have seen Elmek cutting up clerics like so much cheese,' she said softly.

'Well, the best thing we can do is go downstairs and have a look for ourselves,' said Lieutenant-Colonel Thanet. 'They should have brought your box in by now, so our ANPs are all together again for the first time since the war.'

He stood up, and tugged his tunic straight. 'You haven't finished your tea,' he remarked, in obvious surprise.

I shrugged, embarrassed. 'I guess army refreshments are pretty much the same all over the world,' I told him.

He peered into my cup. 'Funny. I thought our chaps made pretty good tea.'

At that moment, the door opened, and one of the sergeants came in and saluted.

'The box is down in the quarantine area now, sir,' he reported. His beret was glistening with snow. 'Very weighty it was, too.'

'Very good, sergeant,' said Lieutenant-Colonel Thanet. 'We're on our way now. Mlle Passerelle? Mr McCook? Would you care to follow me?'

We clattered down the uncarpeted stairs, past the hall where we had first walked in, and along a corridor to the back of the house, where there was a wide cellar door, built of solid oak and hinged with steel hinges. To my right, out of the glass panes of the back door, I could see a sodden, tangled garden, and the dingy houses in the next street. Somewhere deep beneath our feet, a Tube train rattled on its way to Earl's Court.

The sergeant unlocked the cellar door, and swung it open. When I saw the back of it, I gave Madeleine a nudge, and pointed. Nailed on to the wood was a cross identical to that silver crucifix welded over the hatch of the tank at Pont D'Ouilly. Lieutenant-Colonel Thanet said: 'That's what you'd call our longstop, if you played cricket. We have it re-blessed every year by Father Mullaney, just to make sure.'

With his head bowed to avoid the low whitewashed ceiling, Lieutenant-Colonel Thanet stepped through the cellar door and down the wooden staircase. I followed, and Madeleine came behind.

At the bottom of the stairs, we found ourselves in a wide white basement, lit by naked bulbs in wire cage holders. Along the walls of the basement were twelve plain trestle tables, six each side, and on each table was a black, dusty sack. The twelve acolytes of Adramelech, nothing but bones right now, but each capable of hideous and warlike life. In the centre of the floor, silent and still, lay the copper-and-lead trunk that we had brought over from France. Elmek, or Asmorod, the devil of sharp knives.

We walked slowly up and down the room, looking at each of the sacks in turn. Then Lieutenant-Colonel Thanet said: 'Well? What do you propose we do?'

'We have to identify them first, devil by devil,' I told him, looking around the basement. 'Then we might be able to exorcise them. I have the books upstairs.'

'You can exorcise them? How?' asked Thanet. He looked sceptical.

Madeleine said: 'By the invocation of angels. It's the only way.'

The Lieutenant-Colonel's face went tight. '*Angels?*' he said, incredulous. 'Did you say *angels?*'

Madeleine nodded. 'You can believe in devils, colonel. Why can't you believe in angels?'

'Because they're – well, because they don't exist, do they? Or *do* they?'

I rubbed my eyes tiredly. 'We don't actually know, colonel. But it seems to me that it's the only alternative we have left. Father Anton gave me a book about invoking angels, and so did the Reverend Taylor, and they were both well versed in the techniques of exorcism. I guess it's the only way.'

There was another deep, rumbling noise; only this time I wasn't so sure it was the Tube. I looked quickly at Madeleine, and she said: 'Please, Colonel. I think Dan is right. We don't have much time.'

Lieutenant-Colonel Thanet cast his eyes around the basement, and then at our box, and sighed. 'Very well. If you think you can do some good. But I warn you – if anything looks as if it's going to go wrong – or if you attempt to damage any of these ANPs – then I shall have you out of here straight away. These things are government property, and it's worth my whole damned career if you break 'em.'

Slowly, ominously, the lights in the basement began to dim; as if some other enormous power source was feeding off the electricity. I snapped to Madeleine: 'Get those books – quick! They're up on Colonel Thanet's desk!' and then I pulled the Lieutenant-Colonel away from Elmek's copper-and-lead trunk.

The lights dimmed and dimmed until all we could see was their orange filaments, barely glowing in the darkness. Lieutenant-Colonel Thanet called: 'Sergeant Boone! Bring three men down here with Sterlings!'

The darker it grew, the quieter it became. We could hear shouting and footsteps upstairs in the house; but down here in the cellar the silence seemed to fall in on us like soft tufted cotton. Lieutenant-Colonel Thanet touched

148

my arm in the strange twilight and whispered: 'What is it? Do you know what it is? What's happening?'

'It's Elmek,' I whispered back. 'Ten-to-one it's Elmek.'

We hadn't seen or heard the lid of the trunk open, but when I looked down at it, the lid had been thrown right back, and even in the faint light of the glowing electric filaments, I could see the stained, centuries-old silk that lined the trunk's insides, and I could also see that it was empty. I gripped Lieutenant-Colonel Thanet's shoulder in warning, and I slowly scanned the basement with straining eyes for any sign of our thirteenth devil.

Lieutenant-Colonel Thanet said: 'This is all most odd. I don't know what the damned things are trying to achieve.'

'I guess they want their freedom,' I told him. 'They've been sewn up in these goddamned sacks since the eleventh century, apart from that brief excursion during the war. And they also want to bring their master back into the world.'

'You really think they're going to raise Adramelech?'

'That's what Elmek said. And Elmek should know.'

In the depths of that basement, we heard a long, slow breathing noise, like the breathing of a man under heavy anaesthetic. I looked down towards the far end, between the trestles, where it was darkest. For a moment, I couldn't see anything at all, but when I screwed up my eyes I thought I could make out a darker shape. A shape that I dreaded more than any other. The dwarf-like form of the devil Elmek, with his nightmarish eyes and his hideous rustling body.

'Elmek,' I said softly. 'I command you.'

Lieutenant-Colonel Thanet turned to me in incredulity. 'What are you doing?' he asked me, impatient and fretful. 'Who are you talking to?'

I ignored him. There wasn't time for explanations. The basement was beginning to shake like the engine-room of a ship at sea, and I could hear the wooden trestles rattling against the walls and the floor.

'Elmek, listen. We have fulfilled our bargain. What about yours? Here are your twelve brethren. Give us back our priest, Father Anton, and give us back Antoinette.'

The devil stirred, and chuckled. Lieutenant-Colonel Thanet took a step backwards, and tried to tug me back as well.

'Elmek,' I said again.

There was a moment's silence, and then the devil said: 'I have told you before. Only Adramelech can breathe back life into your departed friends. We must first summon Adramelech.'

Thanet shouted: '*Sergeant!*'

A rush of heavy boots began to come down the cellar steps. Sergeant Boone came first, a solid-looking soldier in light khaki fatigues and a maroon beret, carrying a light machine-gun under his arm. Behind him clattered three others, all with those bullet-like heads and young implacable faces that British soldiers seem to have developed through unnatural selection.

'Down the end there, sergeant,' said Lieutenant-Colonel Thanet crisply. 'Hold your fire for now.'

I pointed out, rather morbidly: 'Do you really think that guns are going to do us any good, sir?'

Lieutenant-Colonel Thanet gave me a sour glance. 'I'm sure they won't, Mr McCook. But we have to be prepared for every eventuality.'

We waited for a few minutes in the dark and silence of that London basement, and I could see the soldiers looking apprehensively at the way the lightbulb filaments glowed and pulsed like electric worms. At the far end of the basement, completely concealed in shadows, Elmek watched us and waited.

'Elmek,' I said at last, 'what do you want us to do?'

The devil shifted in the dark.

'We can't help you summon Adramelech unless you tell us what to do,' I prompted it.

Elmek said, in the voice of an old woman: 'Bring down the girl. We must have the girl here.'

Lieutenant-Colonel Thanet said: 'First of all, we have to know what you intend to do with her.'

Sergeant Boone and his men looked at their colonel in bewilderment. To them, he was their superior officer, and nobody hiding in the shadows down at the end of a basement would normally dare to speak to their superior officer with such blatant disrespect.

Sergeant Boone said: 'We could always go down there, sir, and snatch him. Corporal Perry and me were both in Ulster, sir. It's our specialty.'

Lieutenant-Colonel Thanet didn't turn to look at his sergeant. He simply ordered: 'Don't move, sergeant. Not until I tell you,' and kept staring into the darkness.

'The girl's coming,' I told the devil. 'She went upstairs, but she's coming.'

Among the shadows, I could perceive how Elmek constantly stirred and altered shape. Madeleine had been right about it. It was probably elated at joining its brethren, and it was churning through an endless physical metamorphosis in sheer excitement. I saw suggestions of diseased and slithering shapes in the darkness that made me feel nauseous, and when Sergeant Boone's men grew accustomed to the dim light, and could make out for themselves some of the sickening and repulsive forms that glistened and slithered at the end of the basement, they exchanged looks of mounting mystification and horror.

Through the muffling, suffocating silence, I heard Madeleine coming downstairs and opening the cellar door. Then she appeared, with my two books under her arm. I nodded towards the dark end of the cellar, and told her: 'Elmek. It's appeared.'

Madeleine handed me the books. She whispered: 'What is it doing? Has it said what it wants?'

I shook my head. 'It wants *you*, but I don't know why.'

Elmek cackled: 'You don't know why? You can't even guess? Don't you know what that poor girl Jeanne d'Arc did for the benefit of our help in battle? Can't you imagine what befell poor Gundrada, the wife of William de Warrenne?'

Sergeant Boone lifted his Sterling machine-gun. But Lieutenant-Colonel Thanet raised a hand and warned: 'Steady, sergeant. We're not dealing with the IRA now.'

I called, 'What do you want us to do, Elmek? The girl is here now. What do you want us to do?'

The basement trembled and shook again, and there was a low, irritating sound like thousands of blowflies swarming over a dead horse. It was so dark now that we could hardly see at all. One of the soldiers said: 'Christ, it's like a bleeding grave down 'ere.'

'Quiet that man,' snapped the sergeant.

Elmek whispered, in a hoarse, mocking voice: 'The girl must open each sack in turn. Only the girl will do. Only the girl has any religious faith. She must open each sack in turn, and say over it the words of the conjuration.'

While Elmek was talking, I was straining my eyes in the dim light to read the pages which the Reverend Taylor had marked in his thin black book. The section was headed *The Seven Accurate Tests of An Evil Spirit's Identity*, and it told you what you had to do to discover the true name of a demon or devil. But as I read more and more, my confidence sank. The first test was to ask the devil its name by the power of Sammael, the arch-demon whom they called 'the venom of God'. The second test was to burn the devil's hair or scales and see whether the smoke sank downwards or rose upwards. The third test was to sprinkle various herbs on its skin – borage, fennel, parsley, and dozens of others, because different devils were marked or repelled by different plants. The fourth was to spray a silver spoonful of devil's blood across twenty-six cards with letters of the alphabet on them, and the blood would fall on every card except those with the letters of its own name. The fifth and the sixth and the seventh were equally impossible, and all of them were obviously devised for a full-scale ritual exorcism. What we had here, in this cellar in Huntingdon Place, was an occult emergency.

'Madeleine,' I hissed. 'Madeleine, I can't do these tests. They're too complicated.'

She lifted a finger. 'Wait,' she whispered back. 'There may be some other way.'

'What other way? What are you talking about?'

'You will have to trust me,' she said.

'Well, what do you want me to do. You can't go around opening up those sacks!'

'I must.'

'Madeleine, I—'

She reached out in the darkness and held my arm. 'Trust me,' she said. 'As I open up each sack, I will try and discover the name of the devil within it, and I will try to pass that name on to you. These are only lesser devils. They're fierce and warlike and loathsome, but they're not wise.'

'And what do I do when you've told me their names?' I asked her. 'Always supposing that we live that long.'

She pressed her hand against *L'Invocation des Anges*. She said: 'Look up each name in the book, and beside it you will see another name, the name of the devil's corresponding angel. Invoke that angel by repeating the words of the conjuration.'

I frowned at her. 'How do you know all this? I thought that—'

Elmek wheezed: 'Come on, girl, open up these sacks for me! Tear open these sacks and release my beloved brethren! Hurry, girl, there is little time left!'

The basement lights pulsed brighter, and then dimmed

dark again. I could feel a deep, systematic throbbing throughout the whole room, like the gristly beating of some gruesome heart. Between me and Elmek, Sergeant Boone and his men now stood with their machine-guns raised, and Lieutenant-Colonel Thanet was turning towards us with an expression of responsible concern. I suppose they teach them responsible concern at officer school.

He said: 'I can't advise you to do what the devil says, Mlle Passerelle. In fact, I'll have to order you to stay back.'

Madeleine gave my hand a last, gentle squeeze. 'I'm sorry, Lieutenant-Colonel. But I cannot do what you ask.'

Elmek, in what sounded like eight vibrant voices speaking at once, called: 'Open the sacks, girl! Asmorod is impatient!'

Madeleine took one step forward. As she did so, a hideous shape emerged from the shadows at the far end of the basement – a shape like the black glossy skull of a beetle. There was a shivering, rustling, grasshopper sound, the chirring noise of insects. But it wasn't an insect, because I could make out tentacles as well, and some grotesque shape attached to its abdomen like a deformed Siamese twin of itself.

Lieutenant-Colonel Thanet shouted: '*Fire!*'

What happened next seemed to happen so slowly that I remember every detail of it, like some repulsive action replay that goes over and over inside your mind. I saw the sergeant and his three soldiers raise their machine-guns. I saw Lieutenant-Colonel Thanet taking one pace backwards. Then, out of one soldier's mouth, in a dreadful torrent, came gallons and gallons of bloody chopped-up slush, splattering all over the concrete floor. It looked as if he was puking a hundredweight of raw hamburger meat, and Madeleine turned her face away with a mewl of anguish. Transfixed, I watched as the soldier's whole body seemed to collapse like an empty cushion-cover, and he twisted over and lay flat on his face on the gory floor. Beside him, Sergeant Boone collapsed in the same way, his fatigues black with bile and blood, and then the other two soldiers. The sweetish smell was overwhelming, and I had two dry heaves before I could control my stomach.

The darkness, almost thankfully, closed in again. I wiped cold perspiration away from my forehead, and pulled Madeleine back, away from the four dead soldiers. It was silent for a minute or two; but then I heard Elmek's creaky laughing, the voice of an old crone, but a harshly inhuman voice as well, as if its breath were piping through a throat lined with black hairs.

'They dared to threaten me,' the devil mocked us. 'They dared to raise their weapons against me. It's almost a pity that you couldn't see, from the outside, the artistry of what I did to them. But then that's the elegance of such a death. Their bowels and their stomachs and their lungs and their kidneys were sliced up and vomited out, leaving their bodies as empty as their stupid heads.'

Lieutenant-Colonel Thanet, his voice shaking, said: 'I think we'd better try to make a run for it, Mr McCook.'

I said: 'I don't think there's much point, Colonel. We could be minced up like that before we even got up the first step. Damn it, that's why we were forced to come here in the first place!'

Madeleine interrupted: 'It won't harm us, *monsieur le colonel*, if we do what it tells us to do. Now, I must open those sacks. We don't have any more time to waste.'

Lieutenant-Colonel Thanet snapped: 'I forbid it! I forbid you to take a single step!'

'Then I shall take several,' said Madeleine, defiantly, and pushed past him into the gloom.

Elmek's husky rustle of approval made me feel as if my shirt had been suddenly soaked in iced water. I tried to follow Madeleine, but she turned round and instructed me quietly: 'Stay there, Dan. Please. Stay back. Just listen to the names when I tell you, and invoke their angels.'

Elmek hissed: 'What are you saying? What are you talking about?'

Madeleine turned and looked straight into the convoluted shadows where the devil lurked. 'I am doing what I have to do,' she said simply, and went up to the first trestle table.

She stood over the table for what seemed like minutes on end, but was only a few seconds. Then she said: 'I summon thee, O being of darkness, O spirit of the pit. I command thee to make thy most evil appearance. I order thee to come forth, and I nullify all seals upon thee, all ties that bind thee. *Venite* O spirit.'

Then she gripped the musty fabric of the sack, and ripped it open.

From where I was standing, it was difficult for me to see. But I could glimpse strange bones, and smell arcane dusts, and hear the rattle of fiendish vertebrae. Madeleine reached into the sack, and lifted out the devil's skull, holding it up for Elmek to see.

'The devil Umbakrail,' she said. 'The devil of darkness and evil events after nightfall.'

I was so fascinated by what she was doing that I almost forgot to look up the name Umbakrail in *L'Invocation des Anges*. But as she moved to the next trestle, I hurriedly turned through the pages until I found it. Umbakrail, also Umbaqurahal, also S'aamed. The devil of dark. There was even an etching of it – a grotesque beast with staring eyes and razor-sharp claws. On the facing page, in Henri St Ermin's laborious French, was a description of its seraphic counterpart, the angel Seron, and below that were the words which would call down Seron to banish the evil presence of its hellish adversary.

'O angel,' I muttered, fearful that Elmek might hear what I was doing, 'I adjure thee in the name of the blessed Virgin Mary, by her holy milk, by her sanctified body, by her sanctified soul, to come forth. I ask thee by all the holy names: Eloy, Jehova, El Oristan, Sechiel, Laaval . . .'

Lieutenant-Colonel Thanet said: 'What the hell are you doing?'

I glanced up at him. 'You mean what the *heaven* am I doing. I'm calling down the angels to get us out of this.'

'For God's sake, man, that girl's in deadly danger! We've got to—'

I hissed: 'Shut up! There's nothing else we can do! You saw what Elmek did to your men! Now, just give us a chance to do it our way!'

Lieutenant-Colonel Thanet was about to protest, but a low, unpleasant rumbling went through the cellar, and he turned towards the writhing shapes of the demon Elmek in alarm. Madeleine had spoken the words of the conjuration over the second sack, and was pulling apart the soft medieval fabric to reveal the terrifying skeleton within.

Again, she raised the skull. It was long and narrow, with slanted eye-sockets, and the nubs of two horns. I felt a chilly ripple flow out from it, as if someone had opened the door of a cold-store. The lights in the cellar sank and flickered, and I sensed the mounting presence of unspeakable malevolence and cruelty.

'Cholok,' said Madeleine, identifying the devil for me. 'The devil of suffocation. The devil who smothers children and asphyxiates victims of fires.'

Lieutenant-Colonel Thanet glared at me in helpless desperation, but I was too busy leafing through my book. There it was. Cholok, sometimes known as Nar-speth. A devil with a face of absolute dispassion, and the leathery wings of a reptile. On the page opposite, I saw that its heavenly opposite was Melés, the angel of purity and happiness. I spoke the words to summon Melés, and then watched Madeleine as she went to the third sack.

Skeleton by skeleton, from the third sack to the fourth, and then to the fifth and the sixth and the seventh, the skeletons of each devil were taken from the ancient material in which they had been sewn up for so long. As yet, they took on no life, but I guessed that when all of them were free from their religious captivity, they would clothe themselves in flesh the way that Elmek must have done in Father Anton's cellar.

The noise in the cellar was hideous and unnerving. As each devil was freed, the chorus of hellish voices grew louder; until the whole place sounded like an insane asylum, with scratching insect sounds and grotesque shrieks, and voices that whispered incessantly of death and plague and aberrations beyond human understanding. I was sweating so much that my fingers made damp dimples on the pages of *L'Invocation des Anges*, and Lieutenant-Colonel Thanet was holding his hands to his ears in stunned disbelief.

At last, Madeleine spoke the words to free the last devil from his sack – the demon Themgoroth, the hawk-like devil of blindness. In my turn, I mumbled the invocation that would bring down Themgoroth's angelic opponent Asrul.

I didn't forget to call Elmek's angel, either. Jespahad, the angel of healing.

Madeleine stepped back towards us. All the bones were revealed now, and the ghastly skulls faced each other across the cellar, with the distorted form of Elmek twisting and shifting between them. The stench was disgusting – a fetid mixing of thirteen nauseous odours that made my eyes water and my stomach tense in physical rebellion. Beside me, Lieutenant-Colonel Thanet gagged, and had to wipe his mouth with his handkerchief.

The cacophony of voices and sounds was growing, too. As I leaned towards Madeleine and whispered: 'I did it.

I think I did it,' she could hardly hear me over the shrieks and cries and gibbering noises. She said: 'What?'

'I did it. I called all the angels. What happens now?'

'Yes,' said Thanet, his face pale. 'Where are they? If they're supposed to come and help us, where are they?'

Madeleine looked at us for a moment. Her pale green eyes were very bright and very intense. She seemed to have taken on some indefinite charisma of pure strength and determination, as if she knew now exactly what had to be done, and how, and that she was going to carry it out whatever the cost.

She said: 'It is not yet time. But the angels will come. First, we must let these devils call up Adramelech.'

'Adramelech?' asked Lieutenant-Colonel Thanet, aghast. 'But we don't stand any kind of a chance against Adramelech!'

Elmek's voice boomed and grumbled over the screams and whispers of his fellow devils. 'I am pleased,' it said, in a frighteningly amplified tone. 'I am well pleased. At last, my brethren and I are reunited! You will have your reward, mortals. You will have your reward!'

Madeleine turned to the devil, and called back: 'We are pleased to serve you, my lord.'

I said: 'Madeleine—' and reached for her arm, but she brushed me away.

'We are true disciples of Adramelech and all his works,' she cried out, her voice high and thin over the bellowing and groaning of the thirteen devils. 'We will follow Adramelech wherever his chancellorship should lead us, and we will gladly bow before him in the courts of the nether kingdom!'

'For Christ's sake, Madeleine,' I snapped. But she ignored me, and lifted her arms high.

'Summon Adramelech when you will,' she shrilled. 'Let us abase ourselves before his evil glory and his malevolent majesty!'

There was a thunderous roar, like a locomotive at full

159

speed. The lights went out altogether, and we were plunged into a darkness that was loud with horrifying sounds and whispers, and sickening stenches of putrefaction. I said: 'Madeleine—' again, but she called back: 'Don't move! Just stay where you are! The devils are taking on flesh!'

Lieutenant-Colonel Thanet put in sharply: 'We're going to have to move. We can't stay here. We're sitting targets. I vote we go for the steps while it's still dark.'

'Colonel, these things are creatures of darkness. They can see you standing there as easily as if it were daylight.'

'But, dammit, we can't just stay here! One of us has to go for help!'

Madeleine begged: 'Please, Colonel! Just stay calm and keep still! We do have a chance, if you'll just stay calm!'

It was a little like asking someone to stay calm in a pitch-black cage of mentally-disturbed leopards. What made it more difficult was that Lieutenant-Colonel Thanet was trained for action. His whole philosophy of life was – if in doubt, *do* something. He said: 'I'm going to make a run for it, that's all!'

Madeleine shouted: 'No!' and I tried to grab the colonel's arm in the darkness, but I guess he was practised at rugby or something, because he ducked deftly out of my way, and was gone.

We couldn't see them, but we *heard* them. As Lieutenant-Colonel Thanet dodged across the basement floor, the devils abruptly turned on him, their bodies rustling and clattering in a hideous excited rush. He reached the foot of the stairs, and I think he managed to stumble up the first two or three steps. But then he said: '*Ah!*' in an odd, choked voice, and I heard him trip and fall heavily on to the floor.

Madeleine said: '*Oh, mon Dieu .* ' but both of us knew that it would be suicidal to go to help him The darkness was total, and we would have been snapped up like baby mice tossed to a rat.

Suddenly, though, the ghastly hustle and flurry of devils died away; and out of the dark I saw a dim phosphorescent outline, which I recognised as Elmek. It shuddered and twisted, changing through images of bizarre and vicious reptiles to formless squids and threatening clouds of ectoplasm. Then, in a voice so grating that it was hardly recognisable, it spoke to its twelve brethren.

'Leave . . . the man . . . unharmed . . . He is a morsel . . . for our master . . . Adramelech . . .'

Gradually, the lights in the cellar began to glow again. They didn't shine brightly, and all we could see of the devils was a grotesque huddle of shadowy shapes around the foot of the steps. But they showed that Lieutenant-Colonel Thanet was still alive, crouched on the floor with his hands held over his head to protect himself from claws and teeth and leathery wings that had only just spared him.

'These mortals . . . will all be offered . . .' continued Elmek harshly. 'That is their reward . . . for helping us . . .'

Madeleine took a step forward, and the cluster of devils whispered and rustled.

'Is that your idea of a bargain?' she said, in a clear tone. 'Is that your idea of keeping your promises?'

Elmek laughed, and its laugh came out like shattered splinters of glass.

'You said . . . you wished . . . to serve Adramelech . . .'

'And we will! We will be the two most devoted mortals that his malevolence has ever known! But we cannot serve him if you use us as sacrifices!'

I stayed well back while Madeleine argued with Elmek. For one thing – although I couldn't guess how – she seemed to have the situation under some kind of control. Either she hadn't been levelling with me when we first met by the tank in Normandy, or else she was showing a side of her character I just hadn't guessed at. But whichever it was, she was making a skilfull play at keeping us alive, and that was all that mattered.

Apart from that, I stayed well back because those devils, those terrifying gargoyles who lived and breathed and ground their teeth in almost overwhelming blood-lust, were the shadowy stuff of nightmares, and I knew that if I came any closer, I would find out that the nightmares were real.

The devil Umbakrail raised its bony head from the crawling mass of demons, and I saw the dim basement lights blotted out by the narrow goatish shadow of its skull.

'The highest act of devotion which a mortal can pay to Adramelech is to offer life, breath and blood. How can you say you are Adramelech's loyal servant if you are reluctant to offer your greatest gifts?'

Madeleine said: 'I have a greater and more mysterious gift for your master Adramelech than my life, breath and blood.'

The devils whispered and murmured. They were exuding a stench now that made me feel as if I was trapped in a zoo. A sour, dry fetid odour like the urine of bears or apes.

Umbakrail said harshly: *'You will soon have the chance to prove what you have, mortal woman. We shall now call up Adramelech from his sleep of many years, and you shall have the honour of offering your gift directly.'*

Madeleine was silent for a moment, and then she said: 'Very well,' and turned her back on the thirteen devilish acolytes of Adramelech as if they were no more vicious than thirteen chained dogs.

On the floor by the steps, Lieutenant-Colonel Thanet coughed, and moaned. I called: *'Colonel! How do you feel?'*

He coughed again. 'I don't know . . . pretty rough. I think I broke a rib on the stairs. And something's dug its claws into my back. I can feel the blood.'

Yet another thunderous rumble shook the basement, and the devils' groans and whispers rose in a wave of discordant lust. Cholok said: '*It is time. It is time for the summoning.*'

While Madeleine and I kept ourselves back against the wall, the devils moved themselves into a semi-circle around the centre of the floor. I tried to look at them as they stood there in the dense, clotted shadows; tried to see what they really were. But they seemed to have shadows of their own making, actual cloaks of darkness, and all I could make out were scaly wings and curved horns and eyes that glistened and glowed with hellish lights. They were medieval devils of the most legendary kind – the devils that have plagued men and women from Europe's earliest times. It was almost no surprise at all to find that they were not figments of some frustrated nun's imagination, but that they walked the earth with real claws and real teeth, and that we have as much to fear from devils when the nights are dark as we have from muggers or murderers.

Madeleine bent towards me and whispered: 'What you are going to see now will be frightening. You will be in danger of your life. But whatever happens, don␣ panic or try to get away. You saw what happened to Lieutenant-Colonel Thanet.'

I nodded, dumbly. The stench and the darkness were beginning to close in on me now, and I felt as if I was faced with some horrible but inevitable moment of fear, like sitting in a 747 with faulty landing-gear and knowing that you have to come down sometime. I think I would have done anything for a cigarette. I *know* I would have done anything to be somewhere else.

The devils began to chant some long litany in a language I couldn't recognise. It had a curiously compulsive rhythm to it, a repetitive harshness that made me feel unexpectedly nauseous. The basement grew stuffier and stuffier, and it was impossible to take a breath that wasn't ripe with the stench of demons. I wiped sweat from my forehead with the back of my sleeve, and tried to keep my stomach muscles tense so that I wouldn't heave.

'*Adramelech chastu remlishthu narek. Adramelech hismarad yonluth. Adramelech chastu remlisthu narek.*'

At first, there was nothing but this unsettling chanting. But then I felt an odd sensation, a kind of singing metallic emptiness, as if I was under novacain at the dentist. The next thing I knew, the temperature dropped lower and lower and lower, and I had the feeling that the far wall of the basement had vanished, and that there was nothing there at all but a void of freezing darkness.

'*Adramelech chastu remlisthu narek. Adramelech hismarad yonluth. Adramelech chastu remlisthu narek.*'

Now, the walls of the basement seemed to dwindle away, and a chill astral wind blew across us. We appeared to be poised somewhere timeless and airless, and I couldn't work out which was up and which was down, or how far away anything was, or how close.

The devils were still there, though. They were chanting their conjuration over and over again, in their harsh insect voices, and I could feel whatever it was that they were summoning draw nearer, the way you can feel someone approaching you in the pitch blackness of a darkened room. Something indescribably frightening was coming, called up by this evil and arcane chant that hadn't been heard on earth since the Middle Ages. I thought I heard Lieutenant-Colonel Thanet shrieking, but the piercing sound of it was overwhelmed by the devils' litany, and by the endless emptiness all around us.

Madeleine turned slowly towards me, slowly, slowly, like a woman in a dream. I tried to say: 'Madeleine . . .' but my voice came out as nothing but an endless blur of whispered sounds. She shook her head, and half-smiled, and turned away again.

'*Adramelech usthul! Adramelech hismarad! Adramelech ghu-thil!*' called the devils.

And then their dark membrane-like wings lifted wide and stiff, and their eyes glared through the darkness, and I saw with my own eyes the first manifestation of Adramelech, the Grand Chancellor of Hell, since Patton and Montgomery had raised him during the war.

The vision was so terrifying that I went cold with wave after wave of shock. In the middle of the reptilian circle of devils, huge and hideous, stood a dark thing that looked like a giant deformed donkey, rearing up on its hind legs. It had a monstrous head, and a chest covered with shaggy hair, but its stomach and its hind quarters were afflicted with some kind of crusty excrescences, like tumours. As it appeared through the darkness, there was a screaming sound all around it, a thousand decibels of feedback, and the air itself was distorted like heat rippling from a road. For endless minutes, the eighth demon of the evil sephiroth stood there, turning its head to gaze with stately malevolence at his thirteen acolytes, and the noise was so overwhelming that I thought it was going to deafen me for ever.

Madeleine went down on her knees, and I followed her. She shouted, unheard by the devils in the howling noise: 'This is Adramelech! He takes on the form of a donkey to mock Our Lord's ride into Jerusalem!'

'What the hell are we going to do?' I yelled back. 'Even more to the point – what's Adramelech going to do to *us*?'

'Wait!' she told me. 'When the moment comes – we'll act!'

There was a deep rumble, and then the feedback noise dropped off to a low howl. The basement walls began to rematerialise, and within a few moments the awesome Adramelech was standing amongst us in the cellar, slowly taking in his surroundings, and waiting for the subservient rustling of his devils to subside.

I was aware of such evil in the air that my pulse refused

to calm down. It was more terrible than I could have imagined possible. It was a hundred times more scaring than being jostled by hoodlums on your way home, or waking up in the night to hear someone breaking the window of your back door. It was absolute high-pitched fear that went on and on and on and never subsided.

Adramelech turned towards Madeleine and me. I heard a clear, cultivated whisper say: 'Who are these?'

'They are mortal disciples, converted to the ways of hell by Elmek,' responded Umbakrail.

There was a pause, but I didn't dare to look up. Beside me, Madeleine stayed on her knees, her hands clasped together as if she were praying. I didn't blame her. In the face of the demon Adramelech, there didn't seem to be much else you could do.

Adramelech said: 'I am pleased, Elmek. You have brought us together again at last, as the Nine Books of Hell have always predicted. Does it not say in the Third Book that we shall help in a mortal war which shall divide us, but that we shall come together in time for yet another mortal war?'

'Those are the words, master,' said Umbakrail, in a subservient tone.

Adramelech turned his attention to Lieutenant-Colonel Thanet, who had been forced to kneel in front of him by two of the devils.

'And which is this?' he asked.

Cholok said: 'This is one of the mortal warmakers, who has been attempting for years to discover the words which could summon you up, O master, but also those words which could send you back.'

Adramelech laughed. 'Only a blood-bargain can send me back, little warmaker,' he said. 'And each time I am summoned, the blood demanded must be more. You are even more ignorant than those warmakers of times gone by.'

Lieutenant-Colonel Thane aised his bruised face and

looked up at the demon Adramelech. 'Would you really help us?' he said, unsteadily. 'If we struck a blood-bargain, would you really help us, like you did during the war?'

'Which war?' demanded Adramelech. 'We have fought in many wars! We fought at Agincourt, and we turned the Romans back at Minden! We fought in South Africa, with the Boers; and we fought best of all on the Somme, and at Passchendaele, and Ypres, where we did what you wanted us to do, and exterminated a whole generation of your young men.'

'I know that,' said Lieutenant-Colonel Thanet. 'But will you help us now?'

'You want to exterminate *more*?' asked Adramelech. 'Then you have a lust for destruction and violence which pleases me. There is a close bond between the hierarchy of hell and mortals like you, and it pleases me. One day, perhaps, when mortals finally understand the purpose for which they were created, they will destroy themselves no more, and despair no more; but I trust that we can stay that day as long as we can.'

Lieutenant-Colonel Thanet, for one rare moment, looked up at Adramelech like a man, instead of a soldier. 'You *know*?' he asked the demon. 'You *know* why we're here? Why there are humans on earth?'

Adramelech's sardonic laugh sounded like a thousand tons of rock dropping down a thousand empty mineshafts. '*Know?* But of course I know! But why should that trouble you? Your purpose is infinitely tinier, yet infinitely more exciting! To destroy, and to have in your hands the power of destruction! To inflict pain on yourselves! To pull down everything that the works of man and God between them have created! Why should you concern yourself with philosophy when you have such pleasure at your disposal?'

Clustered around Adramelech like fawning courtiers, the devils hissed and whispered. There was a pause, and then Lieutenant-Colonel Thanet said: 'We need your power for NATO. Do you know what NATO is?'

'Of course, little warmaker. Adramelech is omniscient.'

'Well, it's been my brief to summon you up, and ask for your help.'

Adramelech looked down on Lieutenant-Colonel Thanet with indulgence. 'You do not have to *ask* for my help. But you do have to *bargain* for it. Tell me what destruction you desire to be wreaked, and I will tell you what price you will have to pay. The price, I warn you, is always blood.'

Lieutenant-Colonel Thanet looked disconcerted. 'I don't want any destruction,' he said. 'I simply want to have you on hand as a defence unit.'

Adramelech laughed. 'Defence is nothing more than latent destruction! Why pretend that what you are arming yourselves for is defence, when all you wish to do is destroy those who you believe to be your enemies? Show me the difference between a weapon of attack and a weapon of defence! Do they kill differently? Is one less dangerous than the other? You are even more of a fool than I thought!'

Lieutenant-Colonel Thanet tried to get to his feet. 'Now look here!' he snapped. 'It was my work that brought you here, and it's about time you appreciated it!'

Adramelech, for a moment, was quiet. Then he said: 'I appreciated the work of Patton and Eisenhower, little warmaker. Patton had me summoned through the circle of my thirteen acolytes, and he came to me as a man bent on destruction. He wanted the Germans killed, and killed quickly. I admit that he was frightened of us, and that he kept us in check with his priests. But he desired death for his enemies, and he paid us in blood, and we were satisfied. Patton and Eisenhower were both men that I could be proud of. But *you*? What are *you* saying? That you don't want to kill after all?'

Lieutenant-Colonel Thanet was flustered. He was also

terrified, although he was trying desperately not to show it. He said shakily: 'We can't ask you to go out on a rampage of death and destruction right now. There isn't a war. Not like there was with Patton.'

'Why should that matter?' asked Adramelech drily. 'If you unleash us on your enemies, we will make a war for you. A war that you will win.'

'I don't want you to!' shouted Thanet, wincing in pain from his broken rib.

'You have no choice,' said Adramelech. 'Now we are summoned, you cannot send us back without fulfilling a bargain. You have absolutely no choice at all.'

Lieutenant-Colonel Thanet said: 'What kind of a bargain would you settle for? You've already killed four of my men.'

Adramelech turned his monstrous head. 'I would settle for you,' he suggested, in that sinister whisper. 'I would definitely settle for you.'

'Me?' asked Thanet, horrified. 'What do you mean, me?'

'I would find it enjoyable to bite off your head,' said Adramelech.

Lieutenant-Colonel Thanet was very white. He knelt there for a long while, swaying with shock and stress. Even then, I don't think that he could truly believe that Adramelech was real. His mind had retreated into itself, and his subconscious was probably busy reassuring him that he'd drunk too much bitter and eaten too many pickled onions, and that he was going to wake up soon.

'What's the alternative?' he said queasily. 'War? Is that it?'

Adramelech said nothing.

Lieutenant-Colonel Thanet twisted his head around painfully and looked at Madeleine and me. Madeleine hissed: 'Don't offer him anything! Sit tight and don't offer him anything!'

Lieutenant-Colonel Thanet looked back at the Chancellor of Hell. He said, in an almost inaudible voice: 'You have to give me some time.'

Adramelech said: 'There is no time.'

'But I don't know what to do! I can't let you—'

Adramelech bellowed, in a surge of ear-splitting feedback: '*There is no time!*'

There was a frozen moment when the demon was glowering at Thanet and Thanet was staring back at him in terror. Then the Colonel heaved himself up from the floor and made a dive for the cellar steps, screaming at the top of his voice at the pain from his broken rib.

It was Askalon, the devil of fire, who stopped him. As Thanet reached the fifth or sixth step, he was suddenly engulfed in fierce, roaring flames. The spectacle was horrifying. Thanet screamed again, and tried to beat out the fire that shrivelled his hair and his skin and burned up his body fats, but his hands were alight, too, and all he did was fan the flames even more ferociously.

He stood for a moment, a man of blackened flesh and fire, and then he dropped sideways off the steps and collapsed on the floor.

Adramelech watched him in grotesque silence. Then the demon whispered: 'A coward and a fool. Not a warmaker at all. At least Patton gave me blood.'

Madeleine touched my hand. She whispered: 'Don't move. Don't say a word,' and then she stood up and faced Adramelech and his devils with a calmness and a straight-backed self-confidence that I think I would have found impossible.

She said: 'Adramelech.'

At first, the demon didn't hear her, although some of his lesser devils did, and turned their slanted goat-like eyes towards her.

Madeleine said, louder: '*Adramelech!*'

The demon lifted his strange mulish head. He said nothing for a while, until Madeleine had walked right up to his deformed feet.

'I *know* you,' he whispered, suspiciously. 'I recognise you from times gone by.'

Madeleine stayed where she was – erect and unafraid.

'I have seen you before,' said Adramelech. 'Speak your name, mortal!'

'My name is Madeleine Passerelle,' answered Madeleine. 'But you know me first as Charlotte Latour; and you shall know me by another name, too.'

'What do you mean?' growled Adramelech. There was something about Madeleine that unsettled and disturbed him.

Madeleine placed her hands together in the gesture of prayer. She said quietly: 'I was the girl given to you by General Patton in payment for Operation Stripes. They said I was a collaborator, and that I had betrayed the French resistance movement. Only God knows that this was not true, and that jealous friends had given the story around. But I had to suffer for it, all the same, and I was taken to England and put before you, to appease your destructive wrath. I shall never forget what you did to me, how you gave me agony beyond any endurance, and how you abused my womanhood to the ends of natural or supernatural imagination.'

Adramelech didn't answer, but his devils were disturbed, and I could hear their claws scratching impatiently on the floor.

'I died,' said Madeleine simply. 'I died and I ascended into the realms of Our Lord, and into the care of Our Lady Queen of Heaven. I know now what heaven is; and because I know what heaven is, I can understand hell. Heaven is the state in which the faith and steadfastness of the heart are rewarded in the very way in which your mind imagines Heaven to be. Hell is the working of ignorance and self-indulgence against the real purpose of humanity.'

Adramelech said: 'If you died, Charlotte Latour, how are you here?'

Madeleine lifted her head. 'I was reborn on the day of my martyrdom as the daughter of Jacques and Edith Passerelle. I did not know that I was a reincarnation, not until the time came to take Elmek from the tank, and to reunite your acolytes in this cellar. It is only today that my mind has fully realised the wholeness of my destiny, and that, as a reincarnation, I have a heavenly duty to perform.'

Adramelech laughed a torrent of ugly laughter. 'Heavenly duty? You're crazed! You're as crazed as Jeanne d'Arc! She summoned us up, supposing that to be her duty, and now you've done the same! The girls of France are as simple today as they ever were!'

But Madeleine held her ground. She raised her arms, so that she stood like a human crucifix, and when she spoke, her voice sounded so clear and penetrating that I could hardly believe it was her.

'I am more than a human reincarnation, Adramelech. I am a human reincarnation born to be possessed!'

'Possessed?' retorted Adramelech. 'Possessed?'

'Possessed by what?' asked Elmek. 'By man or by mule?'

The devils rustled in bloodthirsty glee. For my part, I kept as far back in the shadows as I could.

It was then that Madeleine underwent a transformation that had only just been beginning when she had first spoken of angels and had taken the crisis in hand. The air all around her began to darken, and she herself became harder to see, until there was scarcely anything visible at all. Where she had been standing was what you could only call an intense black glow – a darkness so dark that I could hardly bear to look at it.

I didn't have much in the way of scientific training. After all, I was only a cartographer. But I knew what I was looking at. Whatever Madeleine really was, or whatever was possessing her, she was now so physically dense that no reflected light could leave her body and enable us to see her. She was like a black hole in space, only she was standing right amongst us.

Her voice rang through the basement. A high, clear, beautiful voice. She said: 'You recognise me now, Adramelech! You recognise me now for what I am!'

Adramelech ferociously tossed his great donkey-like head, and bared his teeth. His devils scrambled all around him, but he hurled them aside with a brutal sweep of his arm.

'*Hod!*' he shrieked. '*The angel Hod!*'

The devils groaned and howled, and retreated away from the glowing blackness. Adramelech himself drew back, but he was changing now, looking less like a monstrously diseased donkey, and more like a black Satanic beast with reddened eyes and a mouth that was thick with fangs.

Madeleine's voice said: 'I have waited centuries for this moment, Adramelech. Now I have you all together, all in one time, all in one place, all in one earthly dimension. You and your thirteen leprous disciples!'

Adramelech roared in fury, and the basement shook. Bricks were dislodged from the walls, and loose cement sifted down from the ceiling.

'I have my devils!' he screamed. 'You are nothing against me and my devils!'

He swept his black, scaly arm towards his acolytes, and the air of the cellar became thick with fire and smoke and the rank smell of disease. He swept his arm again, and we were enveloped in swarms of flies and mosquitoes. He raised both arms, and brought them down in a powerful sweep of destruction, and there was a tremor that must have shaken the whole building by its foundations.

'*Begone, Hod! Out, deceitful angel! Get out of this place and never return!*'

There was another tremor, and part of the cellar steps collapsed, half-burying the burned body of Lieutenant-

Colonel Thanet. Slowly, cautiously, their reptilian wings lifted, the devils encircled the shimmering darkness of the angel Hod, their claws lifted and their teeth bared in an ecstasy of murderousness. I could see their slanted eyes through the dust and the smoke and the swarming blowflies, and I could smell that stench they exuded whenever they were aroused.

Hod said clearly: 'You have no chance, Adramelech! My angels are already invoked! I call you down, my messengers! I call you down, my legions! I call you down to destroy these vile devils, and dismiss their remains to everlasting hellfire!'

I saw, for one moment, the horns of the devils silhouetted against the ultimate blackness of the divine angel Hod. I saw Adramelech rearing in the background, more hideous and bestial than ever before, his rows of teeth glistening with saliva. I saw the whole cellar lit with the phosphorescence of diseased flesh, and clouded with flies.

Then, my vision was blinded by white intense light. Everything was blotted out in brilliance – the brilliance of angels who had not yet attained the ultimate brilliance of total darkness. I clapped my hands to my face, and turned towards the wall, but the after-image still exploded over my retina. Every one of those thirteen angels we had summoned down had *arrived*, in a burst of holy energy that wiped out human sight, and dazzled human understanding.

The basement trembled. I heard shrieks of agony, and screams of intolerable fear. I half-opened my eyes, squinting against the light, and I saw tall, impossibly attenuated outlines of flickering fire; things that radiated energy in all directions, and cut their way through the devils in swathes of light. I saw Umbakrail fall, its strange ribcage cloven open by light, its insides exploding in ancient dust. I saw Cholok's flesh torn from its bones in papery flakes, and scattered in a hurricane of light. I saw

Themgoroth try blindly to flee, only to be sliced apart by an angel's dazzling arm. And I saw Elmek, too, a wriggling mass of tentacles that shrunk in on itself in pain, seared beyond endurance by the heat and the light of the angels.

In a few minutes, it was almost over. The devils lay as they had before, as bones. The angels faded, until they left nothing but shapeless memories of what they were on the sensitised rods and cones at the back of my eyes. A cool wind blew across the cellar floor, and seemed to blow the dust away, and the stench of Adramelech's devils.

Only Adramelech and Hod remained. Adramelech's encrusted feet were set squarely on the basement floor, his gigantic black bulk overshadowing everything, and the grand Chancellor of Hell itself glared viciously around him. Hod, the shimmering black angel, stood before him like an hallucination.

'Hod,' whispered Adramelech. 'You cannot dismiss me. It is not within your power.'

'I am conscious of that,' replied Hod, in the voice of Madeleine. 'But you shall go, all the same.'

'You cannot dismiss me! I shall stay! Only a mortal can dismiss Adramelech, and only a mortal with proof that your precious God once lived! You know that as well as I!'

Hod glowed darkly, and remained silent.

Adramelech growled: 'For what you have done today, Hod, I shall encourage a war on this earth such as has never been seen before. You have destroyed my servants. Well, I shall destroy millions of your mortal charges. Tonight, such weapons will be used that the earth will seem to burn from pole to pole, and the generations of man will be cursed with sickness and disease and deformation for ever after.'

'The Lord God will—'

'The Lord God will do nothing! The Lord God has never done anything, never intervened, and he will not intervene now! I will see this earth burn, Hod. I will see it burn! And then your precious Lord's precious plan will be seen for what it really always was.'

With my back against the basement wall, I heard this booming, echoing exchange of hostilities like the voices that you hear in dreams. I was uncertain at first, and desperately scared, but then I took one step forwards into the light, and the warring beings fell silent, and were obviously observing me with curiosity and surprise.

I said, hoarsely: 'I dismiss you, Adramelech.'

The grand Chancellor of Hell, looming over me in glistening coils of black snake-like flesh, paused for a while to think about what I had said. Then his yellowish mouth opened, and he laughed such a cruel, evil laugh that I knew that I had probably made a mistake. I took another step, but this time it was backwards.

'So,' said Adramelech, 'you dismiss me, you pathetic mortal? You dismiss me, do you?'

Terrified, I nodded yes. I remembered as much as I could of the dismissals that Father Anton and the Reverend Taylor had spoken, and I said: Adramelech, I adjure thee to go out! In the name of God the Father leave my presence! In the name of God the Son make thy departure! In the name of the Holy Ghost leave this place! For it is God who commands thee, and it is I who command thee! By Jesus of Nazareth who gave his soul, by the blessed angels from whom thou fell, be on thy way I demand thee! Amen!'

Adramelech remained where he was. His teeth gnashed together, and he glared down at me with such fury and hatred that I was ready to do what Lieutenant-Colonel Thanet had done, and make a run for it. Maybe the angel could protect me while I got away. On the other hand, maybe it couldn't. I felt lukewarm sweat running down my back, inside my shirt.

The angel Hod said quietly: 'Do you not go, Adramelech?'

Adramelech laughed. 'Not until this mortal produces his proof that Jesus of Nazareth actually lived. If he can.'

There was a long, tense silence. I turned towards the angel Hod, but its black brilliance was so intense that I couldn't see whether it was encouraging me or warning me. I turned back to Adramelech.

'Without proof of Jesus, you are doomed,' grinned Adramelech. 'I shall devour you, mortal, and Hod will be powerless to prevent me. The choice of the human race was self-destruction, and not even the greatest of angels can prevent it.'

I coughed. Then I reached into my pocket and took out the pastille tin that Eloise had given me. I carefully prised off the lid, and held it up towards Adramelech.

'What is that?' asked the demon, turning its grotesque head away.

I held the tin higher. 'It is irrefutable proof of the life of Our Lord Jesus Christ. It is the ashes of his seamless robe, which was taken from him on Calvary.'

Adramelech twisted and shuddered uneasily. 'It's a fake,' he said, in a harsh voice. 'All relics are fakes.'

I felt frozen with fear. But I kept the tin held aloft, and I repeated, as steadily as I could: 'It is the ashes of Christ's robe, and it is not a fake. Christ lived, and these are the remnants of his robe to prove it.'

'*You lie!*' shrieked Adramelech. '*Take that thing away!*'

'It's the truth!' I yelled back. 'Christ must have lived because nobody in the whole goddamned universe could have tolerated a world where you and your devils ruled alone! Christ's life was logical, as well as divine, and that's all there is to it!'

'*You lie!*' fumed the demon. '*You lie!*'

'Do I?' I shouted back. 'Then take this!'

I raised my arm, and hurled the tin of ashes over the serpentine body of the grand Chancellor of Hell in a powdery spray.

There was a second in which I thought that nothing

was going to happen, and that the demon was going to attack me with those rows and rows of vicious teeth. But then Adramelech bellowed, so loudly that bricks and dust collapsed from the basement ceiling in thunderous showers, and bellowed again, and again, until I had to cover my ears.

His black snake-like skin sloughed off him in heavy, wrinkled folds. Beneath that, he was all raw glistening flesh – greys and yellows and purple veins. Then his flesh began to slither away from his bones, and evaporate into sickening, stomach-turning steam. Finally, his bones dropped to the floor, and out from his ribs crawled a twitching iridescent slug creature that subsided on to the concrete and shrivelled into nothing.

For a long time, I stood there staring at Adramelech's remains, and couldn't speak. It was hardly possible to believe what had happened. Then I turned back towards the dark glow of the angel Hod, and I said: 'Is that it? Is Adramelech really dead?'

Madeleine's voice said: 'In this life, yes. We have much to thank you for, mortal. You have acted wisely.'

I wiped dust and dirt from my face. 'What about Madeleine?' I asked the angel. 'Is she going to come back? Or do you have her for ever?'

The blackness gleamed. 'Madeleine is gone now, mortal, just as Charlotte Latour did before her. She is not dead, but will live in another form. Perhaps one day you will meet her again.'

I coughed. The air in the basement was dusty and stifling. I said: 'What does that mean? She's going to be reborn?'

'In a way.'

'Can you tell her something for me?'

'I'm afraid not. She will know nothing of what went before. But she will be happy. I hope that is some consolation for you. She has served us well, and deserves happiness.'

I wiped my face with my handkerchief. 'And what about Father Anton, and Antoinette? Elmek promised that Adramelech would revive them.'

If such a thing was possible, the blackness smiled. Or at least, it radiated affection. It said: 'The promises of devils are rarely kept. Only the Lord thy God has the final power of life or resurrection. But you may know that Father Anton is in his heaven, where he deserves to be, and that his Antoinette is with him. Those who struggle against evil are rewarded in the life hereafter.'

I was beginning to feel very tired. It was a long, long time ago since those two old men had come down the road on bicycles and interrupted my map-making to tell me about the tank at Pont D'Ouilly.

I said: 'What about the devils? Are we ever going to see them again?'

'As long as man makes wars, Adramelech and his thirteen acolytes will survive, in one form or another. A demon of the evil sephiroth cannot be totally destroyed, except by disbelief. The same is true for angels of the divine sephiroth. If no man believed in glory, which is my realm, then I should vanish for all eternity.'

'I see,' I told the angel, although I wasn't sure that I did. I looked round at the ruined basement, and said: 'What do I do now? Is there anything else you want me to do?'

There was no answer. I turned around, and the black glow had disappeared. I was alone again in the world of mortals.

Very wearily, very slowly, I climbed the cellar steps, and opened the door that led out into the hallway. There was nobody around. Up here, the building looked as ordinary and normal as when we had first pushed the doorbell. The front door was open, too, and I could see my rented Citroën parked outside, with a parking ticket tucked under the windshield wiper.

I went down the steps into the wintry street. It was

almost dark now, and it was beginning to snow. I lifted up my wiper and took out the ticket, and as I stood there on that wet, cold London pavement, I was glad of the icy drizzle, because nobody could see that my eyes were filled with tears.

THE HYPNOTIC POWER OF SOUL-CHILLING
TERROR . . .

Death Trance

Graham Masterton

Respectable businessman Randolph Clare, president of one
of Tennessee's largest companies, is challenging the
bureaucratic Cottonseed Association with lower prices and
greater efficiency. But then tragedy strikes – his wife and
children are savagely and brutally murdered . . .

In desperation Randolph makes contact with an Indonesian
priest who claims he can help him enter the world of the
dead. But there demons await, hungry for those who dare
make the journey. Not only do they want Randolph's life,
but are eager to condemn his family's souls to a hell of agony
far beyond all human imagination . . .

Don't miss Graham Masterton's other horror classics:
REVENGE OF THE MANITOU   THE WELLS OF HELL
THE DEVILS OF D-DAY   THE HEIRLOOM
CHARNEL HOUSE   TENGU
NIGHT WARRIORS

0 7221 6124 7   HORROR

THE DAMNATION GAME

Clive Barker

'IT WAS AN ODD DISEASE. ITS SYMPTOMS
WERE LIKE INFATUATION – PALPITATIONS,
SLEEPLESSNESS. ITS ONLY CERTAIN CURE,
DEATH...'

Chance had ruled Marty Strauss' life for as long as he
could remember. Now at last luck was turning his way.

Parolled from prison, he becomes bodyguard to Joseph
Whitehead, one of the richest men in Europe.

But Whitehead has also played with chance – an ancient
game which gave him vast power and wealth, in exchange
for his immortal soul.

Now the forces he played against are back to claim what's
theirs. Terrifying forces, with the power to raise the dead;
and Marty is trapped between his human masters and
Hell itself, with just one last, desperate game left to
play...

"I think Clive Barker is so good that I am almost literally
tongue-tied" *Stephen King*

"Clive Barker writes about horrors most of us would
scarcely dare imagine" *Ramsey Campbell*

"The most impressive first novel I've read for a long,
long time. Touches of sheer brilliance throughout"
James Herbert

Also by Clive Barker in Sphere Books:
BOOKS OF BLOOD volumes 1–6

0 7221 1416 8
HORROR

THE ULTIMATE EVIL . . .

FIEND

GUY N. SMITH

The slowly decaying corpse lay on the bed in the Kremlin. The icy silence of a news blackout lending a chilling unreality to an occasion of monumental significance. For the Russian leader is dead . . .

A shape blacker than the shadows; a thing that smelled of putrefaction and emanated a coldness beyond the iciness of the Siberian wastes.

Lips screwed into a bestial snarl, eyes sunken and staring. Suddenly his powerful chest is heaving, drawing in breath and expelling it noisily, learning to breathe again.
Learning to live again . . .

0 7474 0056 3   HORROR

All Sphere Books are available at your bookshop or newsagent, or can be ordered from the following address: Sphere Books, Cash Sales Department, P.O. Box 11, Falmouth, Cornwall TR10 9EN

Please send cheque or postal order (no currency), and allow 60p for postage and packing for the first book plus 25p for the second book and 15p for each additional book ordered up to a maximum charge of £1.90 in U.K.

B.F.P.O. customers allow 60p for the first book, 25p for the second book plus 15p per copy for the next 7 books thereafter 9p per book.

Overseas customers, including Eire, please allow £1.25 for postage and packing for the first book, 75p for the second book and 28p for each subsequent title ordered.